I0451893

HONOR

BAD BOY HOMECOMING, BOOK 4

KENNEDY LAYNE

HONOR

Copyright © 2017 by Kennedy Layne
Print Edition

eBook ISBN: 978-1-943420-49-0
Print ISBN: 978-1-943420-50-6

ALL RIGHTS RESERVED: The unauthorized reproduction or distribution of this copyrighted work is illegal. Criminal copyright infringement is investigated by the FBI and is punishable by up to 5 years in federal prison and a fine of $250,000.

All characters and events in this book are fictitious. Any resemblance to actual persons living or dead is strictly coincidental.

Dedication

Carrie Ann, Stacey, Avery, and Katee—writing with the four of you was one of the major highlights of my year! Thank you for including me in this adventure and here's to many more!

Jeffrey—as always, I love you. Thank you for the sacrifices you've made for our country and our freedom.

A high school reunion is about to get down and dirty and a whole lot more complicated in this new romantic suspense from USA Today Bestselling Author Kennedy Layne.

Derek Spencer hadn't even bothered to RSVP to his Catfish Creek's high school reunion. He'd been too busy fighting a war in Afghanistan in his capacity as a Marine and wouldn't even be in the States during the event. Unfortunately, one emergency phone call from his mother changed everything.

Tessa Daniels had been voted most likely to do everything back in high school. She somehow didn't think that included acquiring her very own stalker at the relatively young age of twenty-eight. It had stopped being simply annoying after someone broke into her house, invading her privacy. Now, she was actually in fear for her life.

Derek's mother feels terrible that her son has spent almost every waking hour at the hospital, watching over his recovering father. She sets out—and succeeds—in arranging for Derek and Tessa to attend their high school reunion together. Neither one of them expected sparks to fly or memories of long-lost crushes to emerge, but they are not only faced with their newfound passion…they must also confront the person trying to extinguish their chance to rekindle the flames of past desires.

CHAPTER ONE

"HOW LONG IS it?"

"It's a twelve-letter word," Derek Spencer replied, staring at the same crossword puzzle he'd been working on for the past two days. There had been too many interruptions, and he could only stare at the lattice of white blocks for so long before his eyes began to burn. It was better than the alternative. "Behaving or looking as though one thinks one is superior to others."

"Supercilious."

"No shit," Derek muttered, dutifully writing down the letters in the appropriate squares while doing his best to ignore the irritating bleeps and pings coming from the various machines.

He found it best to focus on the mundane puzzle rather than to look at the bundle of long tubes running to and from his father's fragile body. It only forced him to remember that his parents weren't invincible, but thankfully his father had beaten the odds this time. He'd live to see another day, but who would've thought the great Benjamin Albert Spencer could be taken out by a little heart attack?

Ben wasn't a weak man, not by any stretch of the imagination. He owned and operated Spencer's Meat Market, the only full service butcher shop where the residents of Catfish Creek bought their prime cuts of meat, whether it was beef, pork, or chicken. He was old school and his shop stood behind his product. He always took the time to talk with each and every customer.

His father's motto? Everyone needs a friend in the meat business. A friend provided a square deal at a reasonable price, and friends were family. A good man like him shouldn't be lying in some hospital bed clawing away for his life, recovering from open heart surgery.

"That's a wrap." Derek folded the newspaper that he stole from the nurse's station yesterday, immediately reaching for this morning's entertainment section he'd found in the cafeteria. He'd set it on the rolling tray, saving it for last. It gave him something to do to pass the time, while his father slept on and off for most of the day. "Let's see what today's theme is."

Derek did his best to ignore the antiseptic smell that seemed to always permeate his clothes by the end of the day. As a combat Marine, that sterile odor generally meant someone was either wounded or had gotten injured during training. More recently, it was the equivalent to losing a man on the line…loss of combat effectiveness.

It didn't help that he hadn't gotten the benefit of a few days' transition to get used to his old leave and liberty clothing again after being in Afghanistan for the last four months. It wasn't that the black T-shirt he wore was uncomfortable. It just didn't smell right. Of course, there was also getting used to the brand new, stiff denim of his jeans that he'd had to buy since almost all his crap was still in storage back on base.

Damn, he never thought he'd miss those cotton utility pants he'd worn day in and day out overseas. The thing of it was, he'd rather be over there fighting for his fellow Marines than sitting idly by to witness his father fighting for his life back in the world.

"Why don't you go and grab some lunch and leave me be?" Ben pressed for the third time that morning in between bouts of snoring. Derek pulled down one side of the newspaper and gave his father a questioning look. "You've been cooped up in here for four days straight. Go see some of your old friends, or take a drive by The Grange and see Frank. He just turned sixty-five, if you can believe that. It should be his old ass in this damned bed and not mine."

The last time Derek had visited The Grange had been about two years ago, right about the time Frank had installed a hand-me-down mechanical bull one of those city nightspots had outgrown. As a former third place finalist in the National PBR Championship in 1968, the old crusty bull rider even had a plaque on the wall with the once upon a time personality who currently held the title—Frank Dallas, of course. It was hard to imagine the infamous bull rider was sixty-five years old. It was even harder to believe that Derek's father wanted him out of this hospital room.

"Spit it out."

"Spit what out?" Ben lifted the remote control he had tucked beside him, pressing the power button so that the television came to life. He'd never been a good poker player, and now was no different. "I'm most likely going to be released and heading home tomorrow morning. It's not like you need to babysit me for your mother's sake. I am fifty-nine years old, son. I'm hardly a basket case."

Derek studied his father, trying to decipher why he suddenly had a different opinion in the last five seconds than he'd somehow held for the last four days. His dad had welcomed his presence at first, saying over and over again how much he appreciated the buffer between his wife and the hospital staff. Helen Spencer loved her family very much, but she tended to hover a little too much in circumstances like this—not that he or his dad would ever say that to another living soul.

"Mom should be back within five or ten minutes," Derek reminded his father, watching closely for a reaction. He folded the newspaper once more in half and used the clip of the pen to keep it that way. What exactly was his father up to? "You know that she likes to have lunch with you. She'll probably bring me something healthy from The Hamburger Shack, not that I've gotten to eat anything remotely greasy since I came home. Who knew they even made salads?"

"Join the club," Ben said irritably, pressing a series of buttons on the control a little harder than necessary. "I almost attempted to bribe Tessa to sneak me in a juicy steak last night, but then I worried what your mother would do to her and I caved."

Derek tensed slightly at the mention of Tessa Daniels, still wondering why she'd gone out of her way to give him the cold shoulder ever since he'd walked into this hospital. He wasn't so sure he could use the term *cold*. It was more like she appeared preoccupied or unsure.

He and Tessa had been friends back in the day, always running in the same circle, and now she was his father's second shift nurse. She didn't appear too inclined to talk with him in depth, except to tell him to move out of the way when she was changing his dad's dressing or checking his father's IV.

"You don't need to be cooped up here with me for hours on end. Live a little before they send you back over there." His father had turned on the History Channel and appeared to settle back against his pillow. He even waved his hand toward the door, not bothering to look

Derek's way. "Go. Catch up with some of your old friends or something. Drink a cold beer. For Christ's sake, have two."

"I have a nice change of clothes for you, Ben," Helen said after having used her hip to open the hospital room door. Derek automatically stood and took the small duffle from his mother's hand, also reaching for the to-go bag from The Hamburger Shack. It didn't surprise him to catch sight of lettuce in one of the clear plastic containers. Maybe he should take his dad up on his offer to get out of the hospital for a bit. "Derek, did your father have a chance to tell you about Tessa?"

Derek never broke stride as he continued to cross the sterile floor, though that gut instinct hit him hard that he wasn't going to like where this conversation was going. His mother always meant well, but she never left well enough alone, usually tinkering until the soup was ruined. It didn't help that she'd been pushing the issue of him settling down and giving her grandchildren lately.

No wonder his father had wanted him out of the room. Subtlety just wasn't one of his father's best attributes, and therefore Derek also lacked the antenna required to pick up a hint.

"No, Dad didn't mention anything," Derek answered, setting the bag with his father's clothes on the chair next to the side table. It didn't go unnoticed that Ben was shaking his head at his wife, who feigned being too oblivious. Helen knew exactly what she was doing and she was proud of her straightforward manner. He needed to set the record straight. "Mom, you know that I'm only here for one more week on emergency leave. I hope you didn't go and make any plans that I can't keep. I have Marines in harm's way over there and I'm responsible for them."

Derek held the to-go containers hostage, not that it mattered to his dad. One of the nurses had followed Helen into the room with a tray of food in her hand. It didn't smell any better than the ranch dressing in the bag he was holding.

"How are you doing, Mr. Spencer?"

"I'm ready to go home today. You need to tell the doctor that. There's no reason to wait until tomorrow," Ben grumbled, pressing the button on the remote control that maneuvered the top half of the bed upward. He ever so slowly rose it a little more, so that he could feed himself. "What have you got for me today, Jackie? It doesn't look like a ribeye."

Jackie went on to describe a wonderful dish of cuisine that must have been kidnapped and pureed before ending back up on the tray she'd just set down on the rolling table. She arranged it so that his father would have easy access to his food, even going so far as to pour him another cup of water and setting it down on its own round slot in the tray.

She flashed a smile Derek's way—the knowing kind. It was a measure of pity dosed out for the condemned. He gritted his teeth at being the only person in the room who was currently in the dark about his mother's forthcoming news.

"Derek, were you planning on attending your ten-year high school reunion?" Jackie asked, apparently taking pity on Derek and giving him some insight as to what his mother might have done. It only served to make him slightly nauseated and any hunger pains he might have had went by the wayside. He shot a look toward his father, who had covered his mouth with his hand. Was he laughing or gagging? "Tomorrow night is the reunion. Well, technically there have been activities throughout the week, but they decided on a masquerade ball as a main theme. It's all the rage now, and it's been the talk of the town for months."

Jackie Bauer had graduated a couple of years after Derek, but she'd been a cheerleader and was most likely still friends with the same general group of people he'd hung out with back in the day. Granted, he'd played high school football, but he'd been way too busy working at his father's butcher shop to go to anything other than the after-parties with his unattached buddies. He hadn't been the social type and hadn't changed much in ten years.

The men he'd spent time with recently were all Marines and they weren't much for trendy themed balls. As a matter of fact, they only attended one ball each year, and that occurred on November 10th. No matter where he'd been on that date each year since his enlistment, they all had managed to gather together in far-flung places to celebrate their brotherhood.

"I think I'll pass on the ten-year high school reunion," Derek stated, hoping his mother had heard him clearly. "I'm here to visit with my family and make sure Dad gets the rest he needs before I go back to my brothers in the Corps."

"That's what your father and I wanted to tell you," Helen gushed, as if she'd done Derek a favor. Ben nearly choked once again on his cherry Jell-O. Jackie took a step back, attempting to fade into the background as she crossed her arms and settled in to hear what gossip she could share with her friends. Her gaze was on his reaction, recording him as if he were on video. He didn't recall her hanging out with Tessa back in the day, but maybe that had changed since they worked together in the same ward. He honestly didn't want to hear what his mother may have cooked up, but there was no stopping her now that she'd gained momentum. "Tessa wasn't going to attend either, but I suggested to her that she just had to go with you and keep you company since you didn't have a date either. You've been with us every second of the day, making sure your father and I have everything we need. It's time you go out, catch up with your old friends, and have some fun."

Two weeks. That's the standard period of emergency leave granted to Marines like Derek, who had received a red cross notification with occasion to take away from his post in Afghanistan. All he'd wanted to do was come home to square things away, ensure his father was in stable health, and then head back overseas to complete his mission. Focusing on his assignment was something he'd lived and breathed for the past ten years. His life had changed from what it was. He didn't have time to go to reunions and he certainly didn't need his mother to set him up on dates.

Ben coughed, most likely covering up the laugh he'd been holding back or attempting another thinly veiled alert which Derek would almost certainly fail to interpret properly. His dad reached for the water Jackie had poured him and took a drink. He'd had every opportunity to step in and stop his wife from launching this unthinkable disaster, but he'd let her get away with it anyway—probably for his own amusement. What had he always said over and over that kept the peace during their thirty-seven years of marriage? *Yes, dear.* Yes, it was appeasement, but that wasn't the point. Sun Tzu said that you should only fight the battles that you needed to win.

"Mom, you'll have to explain to Tessa that I didn't

come here to attend a reunion." There was no way in hell that Derek could eat lunch now, especially a salad. He reached across the lower half of the bed and handed his mother back the bag of food from The Hamburger Shack. Maybe he should head over to The Grange after all. He certainly needed some fresh air and a beer, but the crushed look on his mother's face gave him pause. Damn it. "You know what? I'll talk to Tessa myself. I'll explain my situation and how I want to spend time with you and Dad before I head back to my unit. I'm sure she'll recognize this as a simple misunderstanding."

"Mrs. Spencer," Jackie said, putting a hand on Helen's shoulder in comfort, "Tessa really didn't want to go to the reunion anyway. You know that she's been avoiding Bennett for the last three months."

Derek caught himself just in time. He'd been about to ask who this Bennett was until the name rang a bell. Bennett Harris. Who else could Jackie been talking about?

Bennett was an unusual enough name that there could only be the one. He hadn't gone to Catfish Creek High School all four years, either. He'd only attended his senior year, blending in with the crowd. The only reason Derek even remembered him was because he used to come into the butcher shop to pick up his mom's order. He'd apparently made a name for himself locally, considering the large billboard sign right outside the city limits. Financial advisor of some sort, wasn't it?

"Well, that takes care of that," Derek advised, appreciating that Jackie had given both he and Tessa an excuse to back out of attending the reunion. He forced himself not to ask what issue Tessa had with Bennett, because it wasn't any of his concern and he didn't much care. He wasn't a fan of idle gossip. In the Corps, they called it scuttlebutt. It wasn't encouraged amongst the ranks. It was time for him to leave while he still had the advantage and the ability. "We wouldn't want Tessa to endure spending an entire evening by being in the same room with someone she has issues with, whatever those may be. However, I am going to take you up on your offer regarding me catching up with some old friends. I'll be back in around an hour. I just want something more substantial to eat. Maybe I'll get that steak you were talking about, Dad."

After having deflected his mother's focus, Derek didn't waste any time heading for the door. He breathed a sigh of relief when he stepped out into the busy hallway. It was always hectic this time of day, especially when people took advantage of their lunch hour to visit friends and family. He immediately headed off down the corridor, not wanting to get stopped by Jackie should she be right behind him. He'd dealt with enough for the day. His father's health was improving, his mother didn't appear to be too worried, and things were returning to normal. He had more important things to be concerned with other than social events in Small Town, USA.

The next week would go by fast enough, considering Derek would be helping out around the butcher shop getting people and operations set into place until his father was back up on his feet in a couple of weeks. He didn't mind in the slightest, but it was time to take a break, have a beer, and take stock. Afghanistan was a very dry place, and he was looking forward to his first cold taste of a refreshing American malt beverage, fresh from the tap.

The Grange was calling his name.

CHAPTER TWO

"**W**OULD BENNETT REALLY do something like that?" Kate asked, picking up her glass of sweet tea. "I mean, leaving dead flowers on your car doesn't seem like something he would do."

"Who else would it be?" Tessa pushed her plate away, too upset to finish her meal.

Not even the delicious smell of Frank's butter burger could get her to eat. They cooked them back in the kitchen behind the bar. There wasn't much space to get things done back there, but Frank made sure his burgers were made of quality ground chuck and they used fresh oil in the fryer every night for the crinkle cut potatoes. She was relatively sure she'd lost a few pounds.

These past couple of weeks had been hell and the local police weren't much help. They thought she was finally losing her grip on reality. Hell, maybe she was.

"I hate to think of Bennett resorting to such a nasty level. I mean, this is Catfish Creek. It isn't some shithole like Detroit. Everyone knows me, and it's not like I'm a Karly Stocker. Now she is definitely someone who would have some kind of fucked-up enemy or even a stalker, like in that movie."

"Karly's list of enemies is wider than her hips, and that's saying something," Kate offered up with a smile, causing Tessa to laugh and relax just a bit. Their common aversion to a woman they both knew whom thought only of herself had often been the fodder of many a conversation. "Are you sure I can't talk you into going to the reunion with me? We could drink too much wine at my house before we go people watch. It could be worth a laugh."

Tessa sighed and crumpled her napkin, tossing the tight ball onto her plate that still held most of its contents. She'd been hoping to avoid the topic of the reunion, knowing full well Bennett would be there, along with a whole list of people she'd rather not see. She'd even officially turned her RSVP in to Karly, respectfully declining the invitation.

The whole matter had been set in stone until Helen Spencer had gotten a hold of her last night while she'd been on second shift at the hospital. One thing had led to another…until she'd ended up promising to attend the reunion with Derek. He was an old friend from high school who was back in town on leave from the military to spend a couple weeks with his father. She was relatively sure he never had any intention of attending a masquerade ball.

"I might go," Tessa hedged, looking away from her friend briefly due to the sunshine shining in through the open front door. Someone was coming inside from out front on the tavern's porch where all the smokers gathered, even though they weren't supposed to, and she waited until the entrance closed before refocusing her gaze. "But you said yourself that you didn't really want to attend. Why put yourself through the agony? It's just a judging contest without any prizes—who makes more money, who stayed skinny, who gained weight, who landed their ass in jail. It's so pretentious. Just say you caught the flu or something."

Tessa had to wonder if there was a way to extricate herself from the promise she'd made to Mrs. Spencer. Derek probably didn't want to go with her anyway. He didn't strike her as the type to want to go to something where most of his old friends weren't even in attendance. He didn't hang out with the nostalgic crowd, that she knew of. His best friend back in the day had been Emmit Atlas, but he'd joined the Army and hadn't been back home to this part of the country in years.

"No, I have to go," Kate replied with determination. Her lips slanted sideways in contempt. "Especially since Anton is going to be there. I don't want him thinking I'm a coward because I didn't attend. It would look like I was avoiding him. I'll walk into that dentist's office on Monday with my head held high."

"Ahhh, so how is Doctor Anton Ballard?" Tessa remembered the man and his arrogance clearly. He'd always held a grudge over Kate's victory as class valedictorian, leaving him all alone with his second place gold salutatorian sash. "Are you two getting along any better, or is the king of the hill contest still marching on in his little mind? You should have just let him win back in first grade."

"He's a pretentious asshole, as always." Kate didn't bother to mince words. Tessa could only imagine what her friend's day was like having to work for Anton. It had to be hell. "It doesn't matter, though, because I'm going to that damn reunion and I'm going to have a damned good time. Besides, Rae will be there to keep me company."

"Thatta girl," Tessa exclaimed with a knowing smile, pleased that her friend wasn't going to allow that ass to lord something so foolish over her head for the rest of her life. "You show him that he can't burrow under your skin. You're tougher than him anyway."

And so was she. Tessa had to stop looking over her shoulder every ten seconds, just waiting for the other shoe to fall. The police could very well be right about the events of the past two weeks having zero connection with Bennet. She tried to think outside the box, separating herself from her life.

"What if someone was just throwing away a bouquet

of flowers that had died during their stay? They could have set them on my car because they were carrying too many things and simply forgot they were there when they pulled out." Tessa tried her best to get on board with what she was saying. The alternative wasn't pleasant, nor was it believable. "What if the police are right? What if I'm making a big deal out of nothing? A mistake or some kind of coincidence?"

"I honestly don't think you're overreacting." Kate finished what was left of her sweet tea and set her glass back down on the table between them. She raised an eyebrow and pointedly reiterated what Tessa already knew about the last couple of weeks. "Your house was broken into, your car was keyed down the door, and your wallet was stolen out of your purse at the grocery store. Add in the dead flowers, and I think you might seriously have an honest-to-God stalker. You said yourself that you couldn't find anything missing from around the house. Did you check your panty drawer? That's just plain eerie. Someone could be wearing your panties on their head right this minute, but I still can't picture Bennett doing something that perverted. Have you turned anyone down for a date recently? Or did you sign up on one of those Internet dating sites without telling me?"

Tessa shook her head, having done none of those things. Maybe she should consider the dating app, though. She had no luck on her own and her thirties were right around the corner. She didn't want to end up being an old hag with a houseful of cats. Wait. What if she didn't make it to her twenty-ninth birthday, let alone her thirtieth? What if someone succeeded in killing her off?

Just talking about the events of the past fourteen days caused Tessa's skin to tingle and the hairs on the back of her neck to stand. The dresser drawer where she kept her panties and lingerie—not that she got to wear the latter much—*had* been left ajar. Unfortunately, she couldn't remember if she'd been the one to do it.

Tessa technically couldn't prove any one of those things had been done by the same person or by someone who wanted to hurt her rather than just scare her. As Kate had pointed out, there had been nothing taken from her house that she knew of. Rae had said the same thing, so maybe she was just being paranoid. The scraped paint on her car could have been by some random asshole who didn't like the way she'd parked, and her wallet could have legitimately been stolen out of her purse by an everyday thief. Perhaps the police were right and these incidents were totally unrelated. Then again, Tessa hadn't told Rae about the dead flowers yet. She might agree with Kate now that something else had occurred.

"I have to get back to the office," Kate said regrettably, reaching over the table and clasping Tessa's hand. "Just watch your back and you know that you're more than welcome to stay at my place."

"I appreciate the offer, but I'm fine." Tessa tried her best to reassure her friend, but she failed miserably if the look on Kate's face was anything to go by. "But I might call up Rae and stop by the veterinarian clinic. I can look at those books she keeps on the counter with all the pictures of the shelter dogs in need of a home. It couldn't hurt to have the added protection and give an older dog a bright future."

"Now you're talking, girl." Kate grabbed her purse, already knowing that it was Tessa's turn to pick up the tab. They always took turns, usually along with Rae, though an emergency at the clinic had kept her from joining today. Tessa hadn't meant to bring Kate down with such a depressing lunch, but it had been good to talk things over with someone who didn't think she was losing her grip on reality. "And don't think I didn't notice that you steered the conversation away from the reunion. I don't want to have to deal with Karly by myself, so you had better get your shit together and meet me there."

Tessa waved her friend off with a half-smile, already reaching into her purse. Her grin gradually faded as she recalled the hassle of having to cancel all her credit cards, her debit card, and replace her driver's license. She was still waiting to receive her license in the mail. This whole thing had been a pain in the ass, and not knowing who was responsible was even worse.

Becky, their waitress, had already set the ticket on the table. Tessa glanced at the total and mentally calculated the twenty percent tip. She'd been about to scoot out of the booth when she realized that Kate was still inside. She was talking to…Derek Spencer, of all people.

To say that Derek had grown into a downright gorgeous specimen didn't do him justice. His black hair was cut short in that military style Tessa had always found attractive, and his muscular frame must have developed after leaving high school. She took that back, thinking back to when he played football. He'd always been lean and muscular, but this…well, it was more than apparent that being a Marine suited him physically.

The ten years since their high school days had faded into swirling oblivion four days ago when she'd walked into Mr. Spencer's hospital room and found Derek asleep in the chair. He still had the same effect on her now as he did back then, causing her heart to flutter at the sight of him.

It didn't matter.

He had his adventurous life, traveling the far-flung world in search of danger, while she still resided here in peaceful old Catfish Creek. This was her home, and she didn't see that changing because of a handsome old friend who happened back into town on leave. They had nothing whatsoever in common and the reason his mother was obviously getting impatient for grandchildren had nothing to do with her.

Tessa couldn't help but think back to their high school days, when just an innocent wink would leave her smiling for days. Technically, Derek had been off limits back then due to his brief yet lively relationship with Mindy Weston. Their clique had all agreed that they would never cross that particular line and date someone else's ex-boyfriend, though there had been some to break that rule, like Karly. Wasn't there always? Tessa hadn't, though. She had always been aware of how much hurt was involved when a girl was made to feel invisible by the boy she'd invested her heart in, as well as the betrayal of the one he'd left her for.

Tessa hadn't truly matured into the woman she was now until her second year of nursing school, though her height had been of great benefit for high school cheerleading. By the end of college, she'd moved on from those high school stereotypes, but had never forgotten the one and only Derek Spencer. He was one of those brooding, serious types. That didn't mean she would stoop so low as to finagle her way to attend a high school reunion with the man through his mother. She had some measure of pride left.

Besides, Tessa wasn't quite that desperate. She should

set the record straight so this wasn't hanging over her. None of this had been her idea and she wanted him to know that.

"I didn't expect to see you here."

Tessa had gotten so caught up in the past that she hadn't realized Kate had finally left for the office and that he'd made his way over to her table. Derek was now standing in front of the booth, obviously waiting for an invitation to join her. She hesitated, wondering how she was going to bring up tomorrow night without sounding foolish.

"I start my shift in an hour, but I have some time before then," Tessa answered, as she shifted her purse off her lap. She set it down next to her, tucking it close to her side. She also kept the bill and her new debit card in her hand, just in case she needed to make a quick getaway. "Please, sit. How is your father doing today? He's quite a trooper."

"The nurse from this morning mentioned something about Dad going home tomorrow." Derek slid into the seat opposite her, his large frame suddenly making this booth smaller than it had been just a minute before. The smell of fried food was no longer in the air. It had been replaced by a subtle fragrance that made her think of a warm day spent horseback riding in an open field of wild flowers. She had to admit this was a nice change from the constant worry that had invaded every minute of the past two weeks. "Do you think they should give him the boot so soon? Those insurance companies are so damned quick to shove everyone out the door, aren't they? Dad's coloring still hasn't returned to normal."

"Jackie was his designated nurse this morning, right?" Tessa inquired, leaning back in her seat so they weren't so close. She reminded herself that Derek was only here for another week, at least that was what his mother had said. "She's an excellent nurse. Your father is doing really well, and I'm honestly surprised Dr. Hayden has kept him this long. I think he's just been overly cautious. It's time. Your father came through the surgery just fine, and his recovery has been exactly on track."

"That's good to know." Derek adjusted the aviator sunglasses that were hanging from the neckline of his T-shirt. She couldn't help but glance down and catch sight of herself in the small mirrored lenses. Did she really look that disheveled? Tessa resisted the urge to tighten her hair tie. She always secured her long strands at the base of her neck for work. It made things easier and more efficient when she got ready in the morning. What it didn't do was help make good impressions. The start of his next sentence clearly made that be known, and she was once again mortified that Mrs. Spencer had talked her into something so outlandish. "Listen, I know my mother spoke with you last—"

"You hardly ate a thing, doll." Becky had suddenly

appeared out of nowhere, giving Tessa quite the start. She did her best to pretend that she hadn't been startled as she tried to smile casually at her waitress. "This is the second time in two weeks where I've taken back almost as much food as I brought you."

"Oh, I think the weather is just getting to me," Tessa said nonchalantly, brushing off Becky's concern. She didn't want to go into personal details as to why she wasn't eating, or else it would be all over Catfish Creek by sundown. Becky was known to talk out of turn by everyone in town. All one had to do was tell Becky a secret and it quickly became common knowledge to everyone who visited the place. Tessa had done a great job of keeping things low key so far, and she wanted it to stay that way. "Could you take this for me? I have a shift starting soon."

Tessa handed Becky the bill, along with her debit card. The ploy worked as Becky cleared some of the dishes and announced that she would be back soon with the receipt. Now all that was left to do was get through this somewhat humiliating conversation.

"I'm sorry, you were saying?" Tessa asked, wondering exactly what Derek's mother had said about her. It would probably be best if she were the one to fix what she'd done last night. "I should apologize first. Last night—"

Tessa's phone let out a ring, the light tone drifting

from her purse. She was one of those people who couldn't ignore such a thing without looking. She gave a rueful smile and reached into her purse. The display read unknown caller, immediately setting fire to the end of her already frayed nerves. This was Catfish Creek. There was never an unknown caller.

"Hello?"

Silence greeted her, and she'd been about to disconnect the call. That was right before an eerie whisper came over the line, confirming Tessa's worst fear. A rush of panic swept over her. She hadn't imagined anything. The vindication never came as nausea won out. Someone *was* targeting her.

"Did you like my flowers? I chose them just for you. Dead."

CHAPTER THREE

D EREK STUDIED THE beautiful woman sitting across from him, instantly registering her discomfort and something else…could it be fear?

When he'd arrived in town and spent the first night in his father's hospital room, it had been Tessa who'd woken him up to ask if he'd like a pillow and a blanket. He'd known immediately who she was. Those blue eyes of hers hadn't changed a speck since that first day all those years ago in school. He'd seen them many times on the sidelines of the football field when the cheerleaders would celebrate a touchdown or whip the crowd into a frenzy to motivate the team. Never once had they expressed panic like they were at this precise moment.

Tessa cleared her throat and quietly disconnected the call she received without making a comment to the caller. She took her time opening her purse and depositing her phone inside, almost as if she needed a moment to compose herself whilst ridding herself of an unwelcomed memory. He resisted the urge to ask if anything was wrong. He reminded himself that she wasn't any of his business.

"Becky's returning with your bill."

Derek had made the statement rather subtly, lobbing the ball back into her court. He couldn't prevent glancing down at Tessa's plate as Becky picked it up in exchange for the small tray that held the check in her hand. Her stated observation that Tessa hadn't been eating matched the small discoloration underneath her eyes indicating she wasn't sleeping too well either. He wasn't going to ask why, and she most likely didn't want to tell him anyway. After all, it wasn't like they'd kept in contact after high school.

There were very few friends from his school days who he'd made the effort to stay in touch with over the years. A decade was a long time to still consider someone a friend after they disappeared into the shadows. He imagined that there were only a few older men in town who even understood who he'd become after doing what he'd done in the name of his country—old men with even older stories of places far away and whispers of secrets only a fellow Marine would truly comprehend.

"Um, I was thinking about my conversation with your mother last night." Tessa dutifully signed the receipt, leaving a nice tip, and then set the pen on the tray with the appropriate piece of paper. She reached for her wallet but abruptly stopped. Had she finally noticed the tremor in her hand? "I'm not sure if she mentioned it, but she thought it would be a good idea if we attended the reunion together. Unfortunately, I don't think I can go due to some previous plans I made."

"Really?" Derek asked, replying instinctively while playing out the hand. He could have kicked himself, but that didn't stop him from going down that road. "I was actually looking forward to it. It's not what I came to town for, but it will be nice to catch up with some old friends. Speaking of which, how have you been? We haven't had a chance to talk at the hospital. I didn't want to interrupt your work."

Tessa appeared as if she wasn't quite sure what to say to his question. He'd put her on tilt, but what she didn't know was that he'd incidentally done the same to himself. He tried to disguise the slight hitch with an easy smile.

What the hell was he thinking, bluffing at a pot he didn't want to play for when she'd already shown her desire to fold?

Derek didn't want to attend the damned reunion, which technically had been a week-long thing for his fellow classmates. He certainly didn't want to borrow someone else's problems when he had plenty of his own, considering his father was in the hospital and his unit was overseas in harm's way without him.

"I'm one of the bunch that didn't really leave, except for nursing school, that is." Tessa ran her finger over the edge of her debit card, back and forth numerous times, demonstrating an involuntary habit. She didn't even blink when her cell phone rang, clearly caught up in other thoughts. He wasn't that surprised when she didn't answer it. Her smile was tight as she finished describing the last ten years in ten words. That was quite an accomplishment. "I bought a house over in the Chestnut Village development. How about you?"

"You already know that I joined the service after high school," Derek offered up, noticing that her ringtone stopped abruptly after five chimes. The call either went to voicemail or the caller had given up altogether. He could keep up this pretense all day, but he ultimately decided that he wanted to know what was going on despite his reservations. No woman should be so scared that she was afraid to answer her own phone. "Mom and Dad have a good thing going with the family business, but they couldn't afford to send me to college back when I had no idea what the hell I wanted to do. The Marines gave me time and possibilities. I could have easily gotten out after my first contract, but I'd formed close bonds with my friends and we had our unit. I grew to appreciate the Corps and trusted that I could survive another contract. I currently have one year left on this enlistment before I'm faced with another decision of which way to go."

"Because of your father's health?" Tessa asked, evidently confident in her ability to reach for her wallet without dropping it. "He is doing so much better and could very likely outlive all of us, so you might want to keep that in mind the next time he wants to throw a football around or chop a cord of wood. He won't like it if you take it easy on him."

She unfastened the front of her billfold and then slid her debit card into the appropriate slot. Her blue eyes glanced up, waiting for his response. He'd been so busy watching her delicate hands handle the leather that he hadn't bothered to answer her question.

"Yes, my father's health will be a part of any decision I make." Derek rubbed his shoulder where his last injury in the field had damaged his rotator cuff. It hadn't been enough to interfere with his ability to complete this deployment, but he could just imagine what kind of damage his body would sustain in another five to ten years. Would he even have a chance at a relaxing retirement after having served twenty plus years? "The requirements of my assignment aren't so easy on the body. Many guys fold up their tents long before they hit twenty. Let's just say I'm weighing my options carefully, just as you're doing with me escorting you to the reunion tomorrow night."

"Escorting?" Tessa's face transformed as she smiled at his use of an antiquated word. Derek returned the gesture, pleased that he could momentarily brighten her day. "Your mother would be so proud that you turned out to be such a gentleman."

"That she would," Derek said with a laugh, tapping his fingers on the table. He'd yet to grab something to drink or eat, but it could wait until he had his answer. "And Mom would be really disappointed if we were both to skip the reunion after all her efforts. So what do you say? Would you allow me to escort you to our ten-year high school reunion? It sure would give the people of Catfish Creek something to talk about, along with months of debate and conjecture."

Tessa's grin faded somewhat when she glanced down at her purse, most likely thinking about the call she'd just received. Derek understood the importance of timing, hoping that he hadn't overplayed his hand. Luck and good timing had certainly saved his life a time or two. Now? He had no doubt that Tessa would retreat and decline his invitation if he brought up anything else beside the reunion.

"You do know that it's a masquerade ball, right?" Tessa asked, almost as if she were giving him one more opportunity to check or fold. There wasn't a chance in hell of that happening, so he shrugged his good shoulder as if that tidbit of information didn't faze him in the least. Inside he was cringing, wondering who the hell thought up such a senseless idea. "Still want to waste your time?"

"I wouldn't miss it for the world," Derek replied with another smile. He had to remind himself why he was doing this, but that was easy when some of the tension eased out of Tessa's shoulders. There was something about her that made him want to wrap her in a protective embrace. This hadn't been the way he'd initially pictured this conversation going, but he wouldn't back out now that he was committed. He reached for the pen on the tray and scribbled his number on a napkin. "Here. Text me your address and I'll pick you up at twenty hundred hours. It's probably going to take me that long to find something appropriate to wear."

Tessa took the napkin and folded it in half. She tucked it inside her purse and then hesitated, as if she realized what had just taken place. Derek met her gaze directly, willing her to tell him what was wrong so that they didn't have to continue this charade. She most likely didn't want to spend her entire evening with people she didn't want to speak to on a regular basis out of personal choice. Contrary to what he'd expected, she didn't say anything else but a soft goodbye as she quietly left the table and walked out the front door of The Grange.

Derek shifted in his seat, watching Tessa over his shoulder as she made her way out. He didn't move from his seat until the door closed behind her, still thinking over what could possibly have her so much on edge. Of course, there was another option that may yield the very information he was curious to know. He eventually stood and made his way over to the bar.

"Derek Spencer," a raspy voice stated from behind the bar. Frank Dallas was leaning back against the ice machine with his arms crossed in front of him. His salt and pepper hair was a bit shaggy, much like his place of business. He was tall, lean, and always had a grin on his face. He most likely had been watching the whole scene unfold. He was continually tapping into the endless stream of gossip that flowed through this place on a daily basis and might have a word or two of advice for an old family friend. "It's been a long time, boy. How is your dad doing?"

The Grange didn't get too busy until after the five o'clock hour. The Hamburger Shack was where most of the born-and-raised residents went for lunch, leaving the chain restaurants for those newcomers who liked the bigger menus with huge portions and even higher prices. As it stood, there were maybe a half-dozen customers lingering inside the bar, especially seeing as the typical lunch break was quickly coming to an end. Four of the patrons left in the place were currently playing pool in the back, whereas the other two were run of the mill regulars. The dance hall in the back was completely empty and not even the overhead lights were shining on the floor.

"Dad's recovering nicely. Thanks for asking. He's being discharged tomorrow morning." Derek took a seat at the bar, nodding toward the taps. He wasn't picky about his beer and would take whatever full-flavored brew Frank kept on tap. "Can I get a draft and my usual?"

"I figured your old man wouldn't stay down for long." Frank reached for a chilled glass sitting in the cooler behind the bar, tilting it forty-five degrees so that the amber liquid had a perfect half-inch head of foam. It wasn't long before the ice-cold beverage was set in front of him. "Ben never did like leaving his butcher shop in the hands of anyone else. Not even family."

"Denny is keeping things running and doing a fine job, given the circumstances." Derek didn't bother to grab the one-sided menu that was off to the side, having already decided that he wanted a greasy burger with all the fixings. His mother and those salads she was making him eat on behalf of his father was more than he could stand. "How has life been here in good old Catfish Creek?"

"Now you know very well that isn't what you wanted to ask me," Frank said, giving Derek a sideways look as he walked to the small, square window located toward the back. "Burger with all the fixings and a double order of steak fries?"

Derek nodded his consent, not surprised that Frank

had gotten his order right after all this time. There were limited options on the menu, and Derek had always been a person of routines. He tapped his finger on the hard wood of the counter, debating with himself if he should continue the conversation regarding Tessa. He could still back out with no hard feelings.

"Becky mentioned that Tessa hasn't been herself lately. I was a bit curious." Derek wrapped his fingers around the cold mug of beer, accepting his choice. There was no going back, and he might very well find out that nothing of dire consequences was occurring. What had Tessa said? The heat had been getting to her as of late. He understood firsthand how heat could affect someone's health, so she might very well be telling the truth. "She's working the cardiac floor at the hospital, handling second shift in my Dad's ward, so I see her often. I'd hate to think something was off, and I didn't try to do something to alleviate the situation."

Frank gradually made his way back from entering in Derek's order at the computer and talking with the cook back in the kitchen. He grabbed a hand towel and picked up a glass that had been in the drying rack, slowly wiping it down as he seemed to consider how much he should say. He'd always been what Derek would call a caretaker, always keeping an eye out for trouble in his community. His eyes were always watching, his ears were always listening, and he was always the original first-responder to step up at the initial sign of a disturbance. He was also very careful with the words that came out of his mouth. In effect, he was considerate of what he repeated to others and careful not to bias information with his opinions unless he was asked for them by someone he trusted.

"I might have heard something about the police being at her house a couple of weeks ago for a break-in," Frank finally divulged, turning to set the clean glass down with the others. He then took his time leaning forward and snatching up another, proceeding with the same routine. When he glanced up, there was worry in those eyes usually so full of wisdom. "I'm told nothing was taken, which is all a matter of public record."

Derek wasn't sure he'd heard right, but Frank didn't stutter his words, and he never broke eye contact. A break-in where nothing was taken? That didn't make much sense.

"I can see how that would be upsetting. It might even keep someone up at night." Derek ignored the sound of the pool balls hitting one another, as well as the country music drifting from the large JBL speakers positioned on high shelves around the room. Something wasn't adding up with Tessa's situation, and Frank definitely had more information to spill. "I take it the police have no idea what the offenders could have been after then?"

Frank slowly shook his head back and forth in response. He didn't follow up immediately due to Charlie—one of the two regulars—requesting another draft beer from farther down the bar. Derek took a moment to think over what little information he did have, and wondered if Tessa's anxiety wasn't warranted. Having someone inside her house without her permission, looking through her belongings, and obviously searching for something personal would undoubtedly cause her to feel very vulnerable.

"I'm sure Tessa has already gotten her car fixed from where someone took a key and purposefully ran it down the door. It's a shame when others don't respect someone else's personal property." Frank kept walking past Derek's spot at the bar, heading toward the kitchen window where a plate of food had just been served up for delivery. He grabbed some silverware rolled up inside a napkin before placing both items in front of Derek. "It's a shame that such random acts of crime happened to the same person, but I'm sure it's all just a coincidence and is totally unrelated."

Derek didn't have to ask any more questions, having gotten the gist of what had Tessa so on edge. Were the multiple crimes truly random, or was a single perpetrator responsible? Frank made it seem other disturbing instances had occurred as well, but nothing that contained violence. Either Tessa was having a run of bad luck, or someone was intentionally targeting her. It was most likely the former, considering that she wasn't one to attract enemies so easily.

This type of thing wasn't normally in Derek's wheelhouse, but he could at least take her to the reunion tomorrow night and give her a break from her worries. Should someone want to poke his or her nose into his and Tessa's business while they were enjoying an evening together, he was more than capable of reducing the threat in a quick and decisive manner. He breathed a sigh of relief that the situation wasn't something worse and gave himself a moment to enjoy the view before him.

Food that contained real meat. Actual real food that he didn't need to add water to in order to reconstitute it or heat in a foiled package with a chemical heater. More importantly, it was food that didn't require tabasco sauce to make it taste good enough to eat.

Derek dug into the savory, juicy, butter burger. Damn, this shit was better than he remembered. He'd been overseas living off MREs, only to return home and live off greenhouse salads with ranch dressing for the last four days. He deserved this, just as his father had earned his release from the hospital.

He hadn't realized just how worried he'd been about his father until now, when the tension slowly dissipated from his shoulders. He could only imagine how his mother had suffered, not knowing if she would be walking by her husband's side as they left the hospital or watching him be carried out to the mortuary's hearse. The least Derek could do was make her happy by taking Tessa to the reunion tomorrow night.

Derek stopped mid-bite, realizing that he still had no idea where he was going to get a suit that fit properly on such short notice. He grabbed the rolled-up silverware, unraveling the napkin and wiping his fingers on it until the grease soaked the paper. He then reached into the front pocket of his jeans and pulled out his cell phone.

His mother had gotten him into this, so she could very well assist him in finding something to wear. Nothing he had with him was nice enough. His mom would no doubt know a tailor who could fit a suit jacket and hem some matching slacks on short notice. What was that old saying? *Go big or go home.*

CHAPTER FOUR

TESSA SHOULD HAVE cancelled. She'd had all of yesterday and most of today to come up with an excuse not to attend the class reunion's masquerade ball. What could she say that would have made sense—*I'm sorry, Derek, but I'm in fear of my life?* According to the police officer yesterday, the person who'd made the anonymous call hadn't threatened her. No crime had been committed. How could giving someone dead flowers not count as a threat?

A knock came at the door, following the initial ring of the doorbell that she hadn't answered. She had been standing a foot away from the doorknob, but she hadn't been able to bring herself to turn it before taking a quick peek through the peephole to confirm it was her date for the evening.

Date? What the hell was she thinking?

Tessa hadn't been on a date in months, not since Bennett. Look where that had gotten her in the end. He'd become extremely possessive over their six-month liaison, so much so that she began to impose limits on the time they would spend together. The night that everything had come to a head had been when she'd arrived home from working a double shift and he'd been waiting for her in her driveway. That eventually had led into a heated confrontation that had ended their brief relationship.

Tessa contemplated making a quick dash back into her bathroom to throw on a robe. She could always make up an excuse that she'd caught a virus from working in the hospital, but then she thought better of it. Tonight's masquerade ball might just be the answer she was looking for. Bennett would be there and what better way to send a signal that she'd moved on with her life than to show up with another man? These past two weeks had been hell, and it was time to make an unequivocal statement.

She looked to her left, catching sight of herself in the framed mirror above the entryway table. The black, form-fitting, sleeveless lace, ruffle-trimmed mermaid gown accentuated the curves of her hips. It had been the only one of its kind at the boutique here in town, and it had been happenstance that she'd entered the exclusive shop the day they'd gotten it in stock. She'd purchased it months ago for a charity ball the hospital had been hosting, only to miss her opportunity to never wear it due to being called in when one of the floor nurses had called in sick.

The only thing Tessa had needed to add to her ensemble was the matching black masquerade mask, currently lying on the entryway table. A delicate lace outlined the vivid black mask, but it was the gold silk thread accent that had caught her eye with its elegance. The touch of color would emphasize the amber highlights in her darkened hair, which was currently draped down her back in large, loose curls. Would Derek appreciate the time she'd taken in her appearance? There was only one way to find out. She straightened her shoulders, twisted the handle, and threw open the door.

Neither of them said a word as they drank one another in.

Tessa didn't know what she'd been expecting, but the sight before her had left her slightly speechless. She'd known Derek most of her life. Yes, he was attractive in a rough, manly sort of way. Yes, she would have loved to have dated him ten years ago. Not all teenage girls got their way though, and she'd carried on with her life. But the man before her was no longer a boy, and the effect he had on her physically wasn't a case of a simple high school infatuation.

This was pure desire, through and through. A fierce heat traveled through her veins to every erogenous part of her body, causing her to reconsider the unspoken boundaries they'd put into place earlier.

Tessa had to remind herself that tonight was nothing

more than two friends attending a high school reunion. Hell, it had even been arranged by his mother. Why, then, did she want to bring him inside and skip the masquerade ball for something much more intimate? She certainly wasn't in the habit of doing that in her past, but she could definitely make an exception to that rule.

Maybe it was because Derek was wearing a black Armani tuxedo that made her think of those juicy tuxedo strawberries that the chocolate store always had on display. It could have been his dark eyes raking in every curve of her tall frame, all the way down to her black Oscar De La Renta knock-off midnight lace and patent ambria platform heels that would undoubtedly give her blisters before the night was through. She couldn't afford the genuine articles at twelve hundred dollars, but these conveyed the coup de grace. She would suffer through it gladly if it meant dancing in his arms tonight.

One thing was for certain—time had been nothing but complimentary to him.

"You look absolutely stunning, Tessa."

"Were you able to get your father settled at home?"

The two of them had spoken over one another, though it was Tessa who had come out sounding a bit nervous. She chalked up her anxiety to yesterday's phone call, turning quickly to retrieve her clutch, keys, and the masquerade mask that matched her black dress that clung to her figure so graciously. The material was so light on her skin it was as if she were naked in the evening air. A tantalizing tingle ran down her spine. Tonight was about getting a message across, but that didn't mean she couldn't enjoy herself in its delivery.

"Dad is resting comfortably, while Mom has been hovering over him every second the day has made available to her," Derek replied amusingly, leaning a shoulder against the doorframe. He was, of course, being a gentleman and not crossing the threshold because she'd yet to extend an invitation. Did men like him actually still exist in this day and age? She made a mental note to thank Mrs. Spencer the next time they saw one another. "I think it will be good for me to be out of the house for the evening."

Tessa met his gaze in the mirror, his dark eyes all but promising her tonight would be good for them both. She gradually lifted the small rod attached to her masquerade mask and placed the beautiful disguise gently over her eyes, turning so that she could ask if he'd brought his own mask when he spoke first.

"Your sparkling blue eyes give you away, sweetheart." Derek shifted his stance while raising his arm and offering her his upturned hand. He was only talking about her identity, wasn't he, and not where her thoughts had strayed? "Shall we?"

Tessa placed her fingers into the palm of his hand, warmth immediately spreading up her arm. She was sure that it had nothing to do with the humid air that had drifted inside the door, caressing her body. She gripped her clutch and keys, allowing him to guide her over the small threshold of her front entryway. It didn't surprise her when he reached for her keys and ensured that the deadbolt was secure. He handed them back and watched closely as she secured them inside her small purse. She knew it to be false, but she soaked up the security his presence exuded.

"Did you manage to attend any of the other events the reunion committee had lined up this week?" Derek asked, offering her his arm as he escorted her down the last two steps at the end of the small sidewalk. Tessa was glad for a chance to catch her bearings as he made small talk. It was hard to ignore his hand that had alighted previously on her lower back prior to him offering to help her down the incline. "I heard Karly Stocker went all out with the festivities."

"I was scheduled to work second shift for ten days straight before the schedule had been released," Tessa replied, surprised to find a silver Infiniti Q50 waiting for them parked on her driveway. He'd even seen to it that he'd backed the car in so that the passenger side was facing them. The green sticker on the back window advertised that it was, in fact, a rental car. "I now have the weekend free, but I don't think I would have attended without your mother's gracious offer. Karly got rather carried away this time. Word about town was that she thought our five-year reunion was boring, which is why she took over the reins."

"When has Karly not overdone it?" Derek said with a smirk, leaning in front of her to open her door. He'd put on the same cologne as he'd been wearing yesterday, once again reminding her of a field of wildflowers on a warm afternoon. The subtle fragrance surrounded her and tempted her to do something more than wash her laundry this weekend. "Do you remember our senior prom? I bet the custodians at the school are still finding red and blue confetti in every crack and crevice. I swear she had a dump truck's payload delivered to the gymnasium."

"How could I forget?" Tessa exclaimed, the memories of those days having been close at hand for the past week. "The principal made all of us who were on the committee stay afterward to help clean up."

Tessa lifted her dress slightly off the ground so that it made it easier for her to get into his car. She murmured a soft *thank you* once she was settled inside. He tucked her trailing skirt just under her leg as she tried to recall who he'd taken to the prom that year. She couldn't remember. Her date had been the first baseman on the baseball team, only because she'd been set up by one of her friends who'd been dating the pitcher.

"Yes, I recall quite well that Principal Christianson

made you girls stay behind after everyone else left," Derek replied, before stepping back and placing his hand on top of the door. He flashed her another charming smile and followed up with an explanation. "All the guys were left waiting in the parking lot for their dates. Christianson ruined quite a few plans that all of us seniors had made at that bed and breakfast out on the edge of town by the lake. Why do you think the bed of his F-150 was filled with confetti at the end of school that following Monday?"

Derek had quietly closed the door after describing that entertaining trip down memory lane. She remembered the principal's reaction to having his truck filled with red and blue miniscule Mylar dots that he had still been vacuuming out at the end of that school year. She experienced a sense of nostalgia, surprising herself. She'd never been one to reminisce about the old days.

Tessa shifted her clutch so that it was close to her thigh, something she'd gotten in the habit of doing ever since someone had taken her wallet out of her purse. She caught sight of a masculine, matte black mask in the console. The sophisticated, carbon-fiber material contained somewhat of a dull sheen that reminded her of velvet. She resisted touching the smooth black fabric as Derek opened his door and settled himself behind the wheel.

"So is there anything I need to know before walking

into this firing squad?" Derek asked, starting the ignition and then adjusting the vents so that she had some cool air to alleviate the humidity. The light breeze made her keenly aware of how little fabric lay between her figure and his gaze. He gave her a wink before shifting the vehicle into drive, once again taking her back in time when that would have made her happy for a week. He was so at ease with himself and her by his side. She forced herself to take a deep breath, erase the tension from her shoulders, and ease back into the butter-soft leather seat. "Who married who? Who became rich and famous? And please tell me no one died a horrible death."

Tessa laughed, which was probably his objective. They both wanted this night to be free of complications. Her problems with Bennett suddenly hit her cold in the face, shutting down her relaxed smile. It wasn't fair to have Derek walk into a situation where heated words might be exchanged or a confrontation might ensue. She wasn't sure how Bennett would react, especially seeing her with someone else. The bottom line was that she was tired of constantly looking over her shoulder or expecting to find Bennett standing in the middle of her living room. She was simplifying things, but maybe it was time she took a stand.

"There *is* something I should tell you, Derek," Tessa disclosed, glancing sideways to see Derek's reaction. He might decide that they shouldn't attend the masquerade ball at all. "I ended a relationship around three months ago with Bennett Harris. He didn't take it well, and I think he's been harassing me for the past two weeks."

CHAPTER FIVE

D EREK HAD TO be honest with himself—Tessa Daniels was way out of his league. He'd known it way back in high school when he would spend his Saturdays helping his father at the butcher shop instead of hanging out with his football buddies, and he was certainly aware of it now. It was one of the reasons he'd never asked her out. He was blue collar all the way down to his bones, and it was something he should have kept in mind. Pissing into the wind would only get his leg wet.

Tessa was a stunningly beautiful woman. There was no denying that. He might have seen her once or twice over the last ten years. Both of those times had to have been after her shift at the hospital, because he recalled her wearing scrubs with her hair pulled back. He'd never looked twice, and not because she wasn't attractive or didn't have a wonderful personality. He recalled that she was quite funny when she wanted to be, as well as had a bedside manner that could ease any difficult patient's disposition. That alone could be quite a talent.

No, the reason Derek had always shied away from commitment had been because he was constantly being deployed to places that most people didn't even know existed. He could count on one hand the Marines he knew who had working marriages. He had no time for something that took so much work—back then or now. Life in the service could be hell on a relationship, let alone a long distance one. Marriage was rolling the dice, considering that over fifty percent of marriages in the Corps fail and end up in divorce. Besides, he usually spent six to nine months deployed abroad each year. His hands were stained, and he wasn't talking from oil or dirt either.

Something had changed for him tonight, though. It had happened the moment Tessa had opened her front door. She wasn't the young, awkward teenage girl he remembered from high school. She wasn't the over-worked nurse ending her shift, fatigued to the point of exhaustion. She wasn't the tender-hearted caretaker who'd nursed his father back to health. Tessa was all woman this evening, and she'd literally stolen the breath right out of his lungs.

It had taken every ounce of his strength to maintain some semblance of coherent conversation while they'd been in the car, and she'd suddenly gone and changed the entire mood of the evening when she'd announced that she thought Bennett Harris was the one responsible for the threatening events of the past two weeks. His protective instincts had kicked in and he reverted to his training, wanting nothing more than to reduce the threat and make sure she was unharmed. He would do well to remember that he was only home for one more week.

Tessa hadn't asked for his help. It was possible that she had warned him so that she could deal with the situation herself, should Bennett cause a scene.

"I hadn't expected so many people to be here," Tessa said loud enough so that he could hear her over the live band inside the conference center. The usual country music he was used to hearing on the radio upon returning home had been replaced by songs that had been in the top one hundred charts the year of their graduation. The familiar tunes brought back fond memories of yesteryear, and he found himself wishing he'd taken the time to get to know Tessa back when they were in high school. He would have lost nothing by simply risking a bit of embarrassment. "Karly really outdid herself, didn't she?"

They had spent the first hour of the masquerade ball being surprised by, recognizing, and getting reacquainted with old friends. They were meeting their spouses, talking about their children, and hearing what paths of life they'd chosen. They'd even run into Grayson Cleary and Jake Davis, who had asked after Derek's best friend back in the day—Emmit Atlas. They weren't surprised to hear that he was stationed over in Germany with his wife and two children. He'd always been the type to settle down, having dated the same girl through all four years of high school, though she had been from a rival school.

As for Karly and her need to outshine? Well, she had certainly succeeded tonight.

The conference center looked nothing like the stark, empty building Derek knew it to be, but something out of an extravagant movie. They weren't simply in Texas anymore, that was for sure. The red and blue school colors had been incorporated into the large swaths of soft material that draped over the tables, with each unique centerpiece being the center of attention by recalling memories they all had shared. The matching flowers were set in glass vases, lit from the bottom by tea lights. He should know what they were called, seeing as his mother had sold candles of every size and description for years to make extra money on the side.

Derek glanced up, taking note that the dark ceiling was covered with twinkling lights. Colorful masquerade masks dangled from invisible lines and gave off a Mardi Gras vibe. The festive atmosphere was contradictory to the formal tuxedos, elegant floor-length gowns, and the soft lighting radiated a rather intimate ambiance. It made for a very familiar setting and somehow everyone else had faded away when Derek and Tessa eventually carved out their own small, private area.

The old cliques had already gravitated toward one another, and the evening was well under way. Derek and Tessa could have easily joined, but they were enjoying their own personal reunion.

"When does Karly not go the full mile?" Derek lifted the bottle of beer to his lips, glancing at Tessa's glass of Stella Rosa Moscato to ensure that she didn't need a refill. It had been the only sweet wine available up at the cash bar. At least it was a decent wine and not something out of a box. She'd already enjoyed a first round and was nursing the second, maybe to extend their time here together. In reality, it was more likely she drank in moderation because they had yet to see Bennett. "Is there anyone else you'd like to see and talk to from the old days?"

Derek was pleased when she shook her head, leaning closer as they continued their previous conversation. He'd enjoyed the evening too much to draw it to a close, though that eventuality was closing in faster than he'd like. He'd discovered that Tessa liked reading science fiction, was a secret Star Wars mega-fan, and had always wanted to go to Walt Disney World to see the Star Wars attractions there. The last was very doable. She just needed to make plans, considering her parents had moved to Orlando over five years ago for her father's career. Derek recalled that he was in pharmaceutical sales—a regional representative or something like that.

"I know my parents would be happy if I moved to Florida, but I just can't bring myself to leave Catfish Creek," Tessa said with a half-smile tinged with sadness, spinning the stem of her wine glass in between her fingers. They had both removed their masks a while ago and he could now study her beautiful, varied expressions without hindrance. "Did I mention I was offered a job down there by one of my father's friends? He's on the board at Florida Hospital. It's a great package, including a bonus for signing on for one year, but I just can't bring myself to say yes to such a big unknown. This is where I grew up, and my friends are here."

"You mentioned you were up for a promotion at the hospital here," Derek pointed out, not that he had any personal stake in her decision. Would he be disappointed if he'd left the Corps and moved back home to find that she no longer lived in Catfish Creek? Of course he would. "Would it be worth waiting to see what happens here before making such a momentous decision, such as moving to another state?"

"It's not so much a promotion, as my name was thrown in the hat for Nursing Director of the cardiac unit. It's a totally different position, with a lot more responsibility and a lot more time required on my part. It would be hard to turn down, and yes, maybe that is why I haven't made a decision about Florida yet," Tessa contemplated, lifting her wine glass and staring at the contents in thought. "What would you recommend?"

"What would I do?" Derek paraphrased her question, surprised she would ask him his opinion about her life. She truly appeared to want to know his thoughts, but he couldn't very well tell her that he'd rather she stayed in Catfish Creek in case he decided to return home within the next year. That would be downright selfish and he'd never mislead her that way. "Having been in numerous parts of the world where war has torn apart villages, towns, and cities…family is the only thing that matters in the end. Material possessions are transitory. They're meaningless in the grand scheme of things. Family is life's sole comfort. I've seen homes destroyed, leaving behind people with only the clothes on their back. And they would have gladly given those remaining shreds of fabric if it meant bringing back one of their own."

Tessa fell silent, her blue eyes studying him in a quiet manner that made him think she saw more than he wanted to disclose. Derek wasn't a difficult man to read. He had nothing to hide, speaking his mind only on matters when asked his opinion. But it was as if she saw something deeper that most people overlooked—his compassion and dedication.

"Why haven't you married?" Tessa's soft inquiry came out of nowhere, surprising him, considering he'd pondered that same question earlier. "Your conviction to family is so strong, I'm surprised you haven't started one of your own before now."

"Life in the military can be rather hard on a relationship, not to mention a marriage." Derek thought back to his childhood. He wanted a solid marriage like his parents, and he wouldn't settle for less. He had a plan to wait until he served out his contract, though he recognized temptation when he saw it. "I want—"

Derek caught sight of the sudden blur of movement out of his peripheral vision. He reached for Tessa's arm and had her out of her chair before she ever saw the body come out of nowhere. An inebriated classmate, one Derek couldn't place, had decided to cross the room by maneuvering around the tables instead of using a more direct route through the middle of the room. He'd obviously had too much to drink and lost his balance, but the weight he'd packed on over the years would have definitely made a mark on Tessa if unintentional contact had been made.

"I'm so sorry," the man muttered, holding his hands up in regret. "I don't know what happened. I must have tripped on something and—"

"It's fine," Tessa said, trying to smooth over the situation. Derek had automatically taken her glass of wine and had snatched a napkin off the table. She'd avoided getting thrown to the ground by this man's inability to keep his balance, but she'd lost control of her wineglass in the process. "Really. I'm okay."

The man continued to mumble apologies as he backed away. His name continued to escape Derek, and it didn't help that nametags had not been handed out at registration. Karly apparently thought it would be more fun for those attending to try and figure out one another's identities as they met. Had Derek and Tessa joined in the previous activities, then the lack of identification wouldn't have come into play as much as it did. He didn't like going into a situation blind even though there were a few people who could easily be recognized, especially seeing as people had dropped the pretense of their masks early on.

"Thank you for that, Derek. I have a feeling I would have ended up on the floor if you hadn't pulled me out of my chair." Tessa had taken the proffered cloth napkin, but the wine had also gotten all over her right arm. She held her hands up in defeat. "I'm going to have to use the restroom before this becomes a sticky mess."

"Takes you back to those wild parties, doesn't it?" Derek said with a laugh, grateful that she hadn't been hurt. "Let's go and get you cleaned up. We can head out of here when you're done, if you like."

Derek thought he caught a glimpse of disappointment in her blue eyes. Honestly, he hoped he was correct. He wasn't ready for this evening to end either and was anticipating that he could take her home, maybe continuing some of these topics they had been discussing over the course of this evening. He really enjoyed talking with her and wasn't ready to call it a night.

Tessa slowly made her way across the crowded floor, all the while trying to dry her arms with the tiny napkin. Their evening had gone well, considering her apprehension over a run-in with Harris. She had finally divulged the events that had unfolded these past couple of weeks, even going so far as to tell him that she'd authorized the police to put a trace on her cell phone after yesterday's call. He feigned surprise and displayed real concern.

Derek hadn't wanted to disappoint her with the fact that it took a couple of days to get that type of trace activated. Her fearless action alone gave her security and he wouldn't take that illusion away from her. Which was why he'd explained to her how she should handle this evening, all the way down to the subtle warning she was about to convey. That chance had never come, but it might be offered now that she'd had wine spilled on her accidentally. It appeared her luck had run out.

Derek spotted none other than the man himself standing no more than ten feet away. Bennet Harris' face was plastered on the large billboard at the entrance of town, so his mug was unmistakable now. Harris had apparently caught sight of Tessa as she made her way to the public restroom on the other side of the building. Where had he been hiding all evening? Had Derek been so preoccupied with Tessa that he'd lost sight of his surroundings?

Derek was disappointed in himself for being so care-less, and he wasn't about to let his guard down now. He took a step back and made sure to grab both his mask and Tessa's, as well as her clutch. Unfortunately, another group of people decided this was a great time to leave the reunion also, briefly blocking his view of his intended target.

When the crowd cleared?

Bennett Harris was no longer in sight.

He'd simply vanished.

CHAPTER SIX

TESSA GRIMACED AT the thick layer of sticky sweet wine that had dried on her skin. This was not how she'd planned for this evening to end. She glanced up in the mirror as she flicked on the faucet. The first thing she noticed was that her beautiful black dress was stained all down the front. At least with the dark coloring, the cleaners shouldn't have too much trouble getting the stain out of the material. There wasn't much chance of a shadow being left in the fabric. It could have been a lot worse had Derek not had such quick reactions, which caused her to detect something else in her own reflection—a flush of desire on her cheeks that she'd not witnessed in quite some time. It was all due to one man.

Derek Spencer.

He'd intrigued her all evening. From the moment she'd swung her front door open, it had been like walking through a time portal. Would she have loved it as much had he paid this kind of attention to her back in the day? Of course she would have, but then tonight wouldn't have happened, and she wouldn't have gotten to know the man Derek had become—kind, compassionate, gentle, protective, loyal, and honorable.

Tessa pressed down on the soap dispenser, lathering the suds underneath the warm stream of water as she thought back to their numerous conversations throughout this evening. Naturally, they'd shared memories of their high school days, but he also told her stories about his time growing up in the Marines. He enlightened her with accounts of his duties during the average day, his experiences on various deployments around the world, his life living in San Diego while serving at MCAS Miramar, and of course his plans for the future.

He was coming home.

Well, at some point in the future. Derek had one more year on his contract with the military, and he was seriously considering returning to his Home of Record (HOR)—Catfish Creek. His father's health was the primary factor, and there were other things that Derek would like to do with his life. Pursuing a professional career being one of them. Tessa wanted to hear about all of them, and she certainly wasn't ready for this evening to end. Maybe they could—

The room went dark.

Not like a bulb burning out either. The entire restroom had descended into pitch blackness, heightening the echoes of splashing water in the sink. She'd immediately jerked her arm away, turning so that she faced the direction of the exit. Something held Tessa back from calling out, hoping that someone had entered through the door and simply bumped into the light switch. Maybe it was because she was subconsciously aware that the door had never opened.

Had it?

Tessa slowly reached out in front of her until her fingers wrapped around one of the handles of the faucet. Her heart was pounding inside of her chest to the point of pain. Her blood was pushing through her veins at such a high rate of speed that red, white, and blue dots appeared in front of her. She was finally able to turn the knob on the other side of the faucet.

The deafening silence wasn't so silent. Tessa tilted her head to try and get rid of the ringing in her ears, hoping to hear any little sound that would give her any indication to determine if she wasn't alone.

She'd let her guard down. Bennett hadn't shown up at the reunion thus far, and Derek had somehow made her forget what had taken place for these past two weeks. How could she have been so foolish as to wander off alone?

Derek, himself, had said that there was no evidence pointing toward Bennett being the responsible party. She hadn't wanted to believe that, because having a name to put toward an unknown threat made it easier to face than imagining the threat coming from a stranger. But what if he was right? Bennett wasn't here and that could only mean that someone else was trying to scare her.

Why? What had she done that someone would want to terrorize her like this?

Tessa stepped away from the sink, careful not to let her high heels click on the tiled floor. Should she make a break for the exit? Was someone standing just inside the doorway, waiting for her to make a move? Should she stay where she was until someone else tried to enter the restroom? Would anyone hear her scream for help over the loud music outside in the large hall?

One thing was for certain. Tessa couldn't just stand here waiting for someone to attack her and not do a damned thing about it. She slowly reached out to her right, shifting her body until she could touch the metal door frame that surrounded the toilet stalls. The cold power-coated aluminum grounded her as she took a tentative step forward.

Her arms were still wet, but that wasn't what caused the hair on her arms to raise. What would she do if someone were to reach out and touch her? What if they had a knife or a straight razor? Tessa's throat constricted in pure terror at what could happen inside these four walls while everyone outside that door carried on as if nothing sinister was happening inside her little world.

Would the police finally believe her story when they found her lifeless body? Tessa covered her mouth to prevent a guttural scream of rage that was just waiting to be released. Why was this happening to her?

She refused to be a victim. She wouldn't just stand here like a frightened doe and wait to be attacked, or worse…to be killed. She used the metal frame to steady herself as she bent her knee and ever so quietly removed one of her high heels. She then did the same to the other heel, enabling her to move freely around the restroom without making a sound and arming herself with two pointed weapons.

Tessa gripped each shoe so that the heel was up and facing outward. It was the only weapon available to her and she couldn't afford to do nothing. What came into play now was if she should make a run for it or if she should quietly make her way to the door, praying that no one was there waiting for her. She chose to go with option two. The cool tile was wet from the water that had dripped from her arm, but she hardly noticed as she slowly began to make her way toward the wall where the exit should be.

She abruptly stopped, swearing she'd just heard someone breathing. She dug her fingers into the leather of her high heels in both hands. Her entire body was tense and ready to swing. It was then she realized that the low rustling sound had come from the fabric of her own dress.

An hour could have passed by, though it was more

like only a few minutes. How long had she been gone? Had Derek noticed the unusual length of time since her departure? Would he come looking for her and save her from a fate worse than death?

Tessa took another step, unable to stop the small cry of alarm from crossing her lips when her leg met something hard. Shit. She stumbled backward so fast that she almost lost her footing, but she caught herself in the nick of time before she ended up sprawled on the floor.

She couldn't take this anymore. Panic and distress had invaded every pore on her body and she couldn't stay in this restroom a second longer.

Tessa rushed forward, not caring that she couldn't see a thing. She'd angled her body so that she would be able to swing her heel should she need to defend herself. Her shoulder hit the wall, but she felt nothing but a small jarring. It was as if she wasn't even inside of her body as her mind only had one goal—to reach the door.

There was only one direction to take since the wall was in front of her. Tessa wasn't sure how it happened, but one second she was encased in darkness and the next she was bathed in light and Derek's warm embrace. She wrapped her arms around his neck, not caring that she still held her heels in her hands. She had no air in her lungs in which to tell him what had happened. All she could do was close her eyes and savor the strength he conveyed, along with the security he provided from all the evils in this world.

"Tessa, what happened?" Derek murmured the inquiry against her ear, holding her even closer as he kept reassuring her that she was safe. She wasn't, though. Why couldn't anyone understand that? Her fear started to slowly dissipate and in its place a fury unlike anything she'd ever experienced surfaced. Her throat had closed off and a burning settled in her chest. "Are you okay?"

Derek ran a warm hand up and down her back, as if to see for himself that she wasn't hurt. Physically? No, she wasn't. But she was mentally tired of being scared all the time and she was emotionally exhausted due to no one truly believing that her life was in danger. She finally found the strength to open her eyes, words forming on her lips to tell him that these incidents weren't unrelated at all.

Someone had been terrorizing her.

The last person she expected to see was Bennett standing across from her. The look of shock on his face at her reaction was just too much, so she stepped out of Derek's embrace to finally face her tormentor.

Everyone had been wrong—her colleagues, Jackie, Kate, Rae, the police, and even Derek. They'd all been wrong. Bennett had been at this masquerade ball the entire time and he'd been the one who'd bided his time until she was alone so that he could intimidate her once more.

Well, his fun time was over.

"You stupid son of a bitch!" Tessa moved past Derek, who had never really released his hold on her. His large hand was wrapped around her upper arm to prevent her from getting too close to Bennett, but she wasn't scared any longer. She was angry. She was furious. And she wanted her life back. "I know it was you, Bennett. I know that you're the one who's been harassing me and I want it to stop—right fucking now!"

"Tessa." Derek called to her, hoping that she would listen to what he had to say before she caused a scene. He didn't know what the hell had happened in the bathroom, but he was fairly certain that Bennett Harris had nothing to do with it. The man had only been out of his sight for a moment. "Tessa, look at me."

"Did you think that was funny?" Tessa asked, ignoring Derek and trying to shrug off his hold on her arm. She was too worked up, and he honestly couldn't blame her. It was apparent that whatever happened in the last ten minutes was enough for her to confront who she thought was responsible. Only she was wrong. "What kind of sick individual are you that you would—"

"That's enough." Derek stepped in front of her, forcing Tessa to look him in the eye and hear him out before they gathered any more spectators. This confrontation would be the talk of the town come Monday morning. "Whatever happened in there, Bennett wasn't responsible."

"Derek, he is standing right here. I know he's the one that—"

"I spotted him the second you left our table," Derek revealed, holding up a hand when Bennett tried to intervene to defend himself. The man could have his say in a minute, but not before Derek had a chance to give the facts to Tessa. "I gathered your belongings and immediately sought him out. He was glued to the side of his date this entire time, Tessa. He didn't do whatever it is you think he did. What happened?"

Derek had originally given his opinion on Harris before they even walked into this conference center. It didn't make sense for Bennett to be the one responsible. One, the minor offenses he'd had in his past were juvenile, and the man didn't strike Derek as stooping to that kind of immature level. Two, what would be the purpose of committing these types of acts? It didn't make sense if he wanted her back, and Derek was concerned Tessa would get hurt because all her attention was on Harris—not the real culprit. And that's almost what happened here.

"Tessa, I know I didn't handle the end of our relationship that well, but I would never do anything to hurt you." Bennett had come to stand beside them, his date practically attaching herself to his arm while displaying a self-satisfied smirk. Derek's first thought was that Harris might not be the one responsible, but that didn't mean this maniacal-looking femme fatale didn't have it in her to torment the ex of her current lover. "What happened to you in there?"

Derek wanted to know the answer to that question as well, but he wasn't going to grill her in front of her former suitor or their old classmates. He could easily see that she wanted to hurt Bennett as much as she thought he'd hurt her. That would solve nothing, and it definitely wouldn't help in figuring out who the responsible party was who had been terrorizing her. He should never have allowed her to go to the restroom unescorted when it was obvious that someone had wanted to scare her all evening.

Scare being the operative word. Had someone wanted to actually harm Tessa, they had more than enough opportunity to do so over these past two weeks. Someone was out to frighten her and make her life unbearable. They needed to figure out who that someone was before these non-violent acts escalated into something more physical.

"I'd like to leave," Tessa whispered, her words practically blending with the loud music still coming from the large speakers. She was holding her high heels close to her chest, though he was relieved to see that she wasn't embarrassed by what had taken place. She was angry. "I need some fresh air."

"Tessa, why would you think—"

"I'm sure you can come up with an answer to that one all by yourself, Harris." Derek had made sure he'd remained in between Tessa and Bennett. She'd already dealt with something that had truly upset her, and he would damn well see to it that nothing else happened on his watch. He blamed himself that this was how her evening had come to an end. He wasn't about to let Harris do any more damage. "Enough. I suggest you leave this matter alone. She told me how you started to tell her what she could and couldn't wear, and how you would be waiting at home for her after a shift to confirm she wasn't going out with friends for a drink. Let me tell you something. You so much as look at her with hostile intent, and I'll be the one making sure you understand the word *enough*. Do I make myself perfectly clear?"

"Bennett, just tell him that she means nothing to you anymore," the blonde woman urged in a rather nasally tone, her green eyes all but shooting daggers Tessa's way. Had Derek not seen her glued to Bennett's side for the last ten minutes, he would have actually considered that this woman had something to do with whatever had happened to Tessa. "Tell him."

"Claudia, just stop your nagging," Bennett warned, pulling his arm out of her grasp before trying to take another step toward Tessa. Derek shifted his body and made sure Harris understood him this time.

"One more advance and your face won't be matching that pretty billboard picture anymore." Derek waited for Harris to recognize that he'd pushed too far. "I asked you once already. Do you understand me?"

"Yes, yes, I understand," Bennett said, both hands up in the air as if to ask for forgiveness. "But I haven't done anything, nor would I ever."

"I hear you," Derek shared, resting a hand on Tessa's lower back as she started to take a step toward the front entrance. Only a handful of classmates had overheard the heated exchange of words between Tessa and Bennett, but it was enough that word would get around town. "Now stop before you're in the back of a patrol car, heading to jail for misdemeanor harassment. Do yourself a favor and steer clear of Tessa for the foreseeable future. I don't want to think I made a mistake by letting you off with a warning. You're a smart guy, Bennett. Don't push her any further toward that inevitable restraining order, or your business might suffer."

Derek guided Tessa through the thinning crowd, reading her body posture. She'd reached her limit on what she could take from her tormentor, and she was ready to fight back. He'd never been so glad for the additional week he'd taken to be home, because he would be right by her side every step of the way. She wouldn't have to deal with this on her own.

CHAPTER SEVEN

TESSA MANAGED TO finally lift her cup of tea without causing the warm liquid to spill over the side. She wasn't so sure if it was due to the adrenaline leaving her system or the deep-seated anger that had set in upon recognizing the culprit who had been standing right outside the restroom door.

"How can you be so damn sure that it wasn't Bennett?" Tessa asked, raising her gaze so she didn't miss any of Derek's facial expressions. Something she noticed since yesterday was that his tone of voice rarely changed under any circumstance, making it hard to tell what he was thinking unless she was looking directly at him. Even then, it was only when his eyes darkened that indicated his change of intensity. "How long was he out of your sight before you saw him again? Or that snake he had on his arm, for that matter? It would have taken no more than five seconds for either one of them to reach into the restroom and turn off the light."

Tessa tried to put that simple action into perspective. All someone had done was flip off the light switch, possibly as a joke. No one had tried to harm her, and no crime had been committed. Once again, she was left wondering if she'd made something out of nothing—a mountain out of a mole hill.

"Harris wasn't anywhere near that restroom, Tessa." Derek had removed his tuxedo jacket over an hour ago, when they'd entered her modest home. He'd loosened his bowtie so that both ends were hanging loose underneath his undone collar, and he'd also rolled up his sleeves twice so that they fell halfway up his forearms. He looked comfortable, like he intended to stay for a while. She hadn't conveyed her gratitude. In fact, she hadn't said a thing on that subject. She just knew that she wasn't ready to be left alone. "That's not to say that he didn't have someone else pull that type of juvenile bullshit stunt, just like you said."

"But you don't think he had anything to do with it, do you?" Tessa speculated, not having to go that far out on the ledge to guess what he was thinking. She tucked a flyaway strand that had come loose from the pile of hair she'd secured with a hair tie before she'd taken a shower. It had taken her less than ten minutes tops to quickly wash off the dried wine that had been stuck to her skin and stained her dress. Speaking of which, her outfit was still soaking wet. She could admit to being rather surprised upon finding a hot cup of her favorite tea waiting for her when she'd returned to the living room.

"Do you know how humiliating it would be for me to think that I overreacted to nothing more than an accident or preprogrammed timer kicking off the lights?"

"Had someone hit the light switch by mistake upon entering that restroom, they would have immediately flipped the switch back on. It was more than apparent that it was done with malicious intent, but what would someone have to gain by doing that stupid stunt?" Derek asked, resting his elbows on his knees as he leaned forward in the overstuffed chair. "Someone has been making your life very difficult, and these are very targeted attacks. Whoever it is had to be observing your movements."

"But why?" The delicious tea he'd made her did nothing to quell the frustration welling inside of her. She uncurled herself from the couch and set her cup down on the coffee table in case she lost her composure and threw it across the room. "There is only one person that I've upset to any degree within the last three months, and that's Bennett Harris. Technically, I haven't gone off on anyone in years, not since a patient tried to cop a feel when I was giving him a sponge bath. He was ninety-one years old at the time and died shortly afterward, so I can pretty much guarantee that he wouldn't have had the strength to pull some of these stunts off with much success. Derek, no one else would have reason to want to hurt me. None who I have any clue about."

"But whoever is doing this isn't physically hurting you," Derek pointed out, rubbing his fingers across his chin as he contemplated her troubles. And it was a disturbing act, but it wasn't like she could call the police and expect any kind of real action from them. A threatening call was one thing, but someone turning the light off in a restroom? They would have laughed her out of the station. "It's like they are purposefully causing you to be constantly on alert for something else to happen. He or she wants to keep you on edge and try to put you off your game."

"I haven't done anything to anyone," Tessa said forcefully, wishing she could remember one thing she might have done that would have upset someone.

"You haven't lost a patient you were primary on in the last two months or so?" Derek was reaching, but she could understand why. Sometimes families didn't take losing their loved ones without needing to blame someone for their loss. Of course that had happened a time or two in her past career, but she'd never had any of them upset enough to seek her out where she lived or to make her life a living hell. "Did you cut someone off in a parking lot or flip someone the bird? I know it's a stretch, but you're going to have to start thinking outside the box."

He'd left his sentence to hang for just a little bit too long, like he wanted to add something to his statement.

Something like, b*efore this turns into something more than innocuous acts that were merely psychological.*

"This is Catfish Creek, Derek," Tessa reminded him, staring off into space as she tried to think of what she could have done to upset someone. Absolutely nothing came to mind. "Everyone knows everyone else's business. Wouldn't someone have noticed something?"

The grandfather clock in the corner of her living room began to chime, indicating that the midnight hour had just arrived. Tessa was tired, but she couldn't bring herself to end this evening. To do so would be to bid Derek goodnight, and his presence was the only thing keeping her grounded. She'd been floating through the days these past two weeks, going through the motions while constantly looking over her shoulder. It was nice to have someone else have her back, even for only one evening.

"You're second guessing yourself about your tiniest moves, and that is exactly what this person wants." Derek slowly stood, prompting Tessa to do the same. She twisted her fingers together as she tried to think of something to say that would delay his departure. "Look, why don't you go and get some rest. I can—"

"Stay here with me."

The plea practically fell off her lips. She took a step forward to still his hand from reaching for his jacket that he'd laid over the back of the loveseat. His dark gaze met hers, but she never wavered her stare. She needed him to hold her, if only for tonight.

"You don't mean that," Derek said softly with a shake of his head. He lifted a hand and drew the back of his fingers subtly down her cheek. She couldn't even say if the warmth of his skin touched hers, yet he'd left behind a streak of fire as he dropped his hand. "You're just scared. You—"

"I want you to stay here with me, Derek." Tessa slowly closed the distance between them, bringing up her hands so that they rested on either side of his waist. She peered up at him through her lashes so that he could see the honesty within her request. "I need this. I need you tonight. I need to feel something other than uncertainty and fear. If you're worried I'm asking for tomorrow too, I'm not. We both understand each other's responsibilities. I know you have to go back to your Marines, but please give me tonight."

Derek's jawline tensed until the cord of muscle was visible, indicating he was considering the ramifications of such an invitation. She gently lifted her right hand until her palm curled around the back of his neck, the silkiness of his short, cropped hair at the edge of her fingertips. She lifted on her tiptoes until their lips were mere inches apart.

"One night, Derek," Tessa whispered, something inside of her screaming that he wouldn't return if he walked out her front door. She didn't want a vague phone call tomorrow asking how she was or for there to be an elusive offer to help when there was nothing anyone could do about her plight. There was no proof that these strings of incidents were related, and she might very well be losing her mind. If that were the case, she wanted to lose her sanity over something worth it. "Please stay."

DEREK HAD EVERY intention of walking out of Tessa's house and being the gentleman he'd been raised to be, keeping the promise he'd made to himself not to get too involved in her personal affairs only to end up having to walk away from her.

He'd known earlier this evening that she was different from the rest. He'd reminded himself over and over that he had one more year before he had to make another decision that would affect the next four years of his life. He'd told himself that he would see to it that she was safe in her home, maybe even put a call in to the police about having them do patrol sweeps through the area. He couldn't leave her unprotected, but he also had a duty to protect himself from damaging his heart.

Now?

Tessa's supple curves against his body and her lips inches from his made leaving difficult. Hell, she made it all but impossible.

Derek wrapped an arm around her waist and eased her toward him, not stopping until the only thing that separated them were the clothes on their bodies. He captured her lips, unable to get enough of her. The sweet taste of sugar and cream made him think that the addictive taste had nothing to do with her tea and everything to do with the fact that she was a hypnotic aphrodisiac. He no longer cared what tomorrow would bring. They were living in the moment.

Tessa used his body as leverage as she raised herself higher onto her tiptoes to deepen their kiss. She didn't have to worry, because he didn't intend on stopping anytime soon. He easily hoisted her up so that her long legs were wrapped around his waist, already accepting that they weren't going to make it to her bedroom…at least for the first round.

Derek sidestepped the coffee table until they both toppled onto the couch. He pulled his lips from hers so that he could see for himself that she understood the ground rules that she'd already put into place. He ignored the fact that he was repeating her words for his sake only.

"For tonight then."

"Agreed," Tessa said breathlessly, already reaching for the unfastened bowtie hanging around his neck. She gradually slid the material out from under his lapel, never once breaking eye contact. "So make it your best effort, Derek."

Tessa's challenge was a reckless streak of provocation that immediately raised the heat level. He couldn't resist leaning down and running his tongue across her lower lip, only to then nip it with his teeth. She still had her legs wrapped around him with apparently no intention of letting him go. He had other plans though. He'd become rigid as a board the moment she'd whispered the word *stay*.

Derek leaned up and all but forced her to relax her hold on him. She was taking in every move he made. She'd already removed his bowtie, so unfastening the rest of the buttons on his shirt was done with ease. Everything she felt was displayed across her beautiful features and he had to question on whether the desire burning within those baby blues of hers could literally light a fire in something other than his soul.

"Don't stop now," Tessa urged in what could only be described as a purr. She was full of contradictions, because this was not the nurse who had taken care of his father. She was every bit the passionate, irresistible woman he'd recognized at the door first thing this evening. She happened to be tossing his bowtie onto the floor, signifying her surrender. He had just started to remove his shirt when she reached for the hem of the top she'd changed into earlier. She pulled on the bottom edge and then drew the soft material over her head, causing some of those beautiful strands to come loose from the haphazard bun. Her sensual smile all but caused his heart to stop beating. He couldn't think back to when another woman had ever had this type of effect on him. "You're making my teenage dreams come true, Derek Spencer."

Derek couldn't prevent himself from giving her a half smile at the thought of their innocence back then. The things he'd learned over the last ten years had him very grateful that they hadn't been those fumbling teenagers who thought they knew everything…and he didn't mind teaching her a few things that would have had the young, naïve Tessa running in the other direction once upon a time.

The swells of her breasts weren't contained in a con-stricting bra. They were exposed for his viewing pleasure and he took his time memorizing the sensual hue of her porcelain skin, noticing her hardened nipples were the perfect size. He finished removing his shirt, dropping the starched fabric onto the floor. He then stroked his fingers up her abdomen, into a semi-half circle around her right breast. He didn't go near her nipple, and yet it somehow hardened even more.

Tessa had closed her eyes, breathing in deep enough to cause her chest to rise. The flyaway strands made her look like an angel and he was helpless not to touch.

There was no rush. They had all night, so he took his time exploring every inch of her exposed skin until she finally grabbed ahold of his wrist. He'd been so busy watching her body respond to him that he hadn't noticed she was doing the same.

"Touch me, Derek."

Tessa had moved his hand so that his palm rested against the side of her right breast, but it was clear she hadn't expected him to grant her wish. Her lips parted when his thumb caressed her hardened nipple. The nub was so tight from anticipation that he could only imagine how sensitive she was to the contact.

"The way you respond…" Derek leaned forward, pressing his lips against her warm flesh where his thumb had been. He slowly circled his tongue around her areola, once again steering clear of where she really wanted his attention. "I want all these clothes off you."

Derek pulled back without giving Tessa what she wanted, her protest forming on her lips. He didn't give her time to say anything as he slid his fingers inside the waistband of the shorts she'd put on after her shower, drawing them down her legs as he shifted his body to untangle her hold on him. He changed his mind. The light pink thong with its damp triangle she was wearing would have to stay on her just a little while longer.

He took her ankle in his hand, pressing his lips right above where his fingers had wrapped around her soft skin. He took his time savoring the taste of her as he ran his tongue down the side of her leg, only stopping to lightly bite her inner thigh when she tried to grab his shoulders. He wasn't going to allow her to rush this. As she said earlier, they had tonight.

"Don't move this leg," Derek warned, resting her left leg on top of the cushion as he settled in between her thighs. He wanted to continue his exploration, but he lightly stroked the back of his fingers over the silky material of her clinging panties. He traced the edge all the way down until the fabric shifted. "You're so fucking wet."

Tessa cried out in pleasure when Derek ever so slowly drew his finger down her folds, savoring her arousal. She was so ready for him, but he wouldn't rush this. He let the pink lace of her panties fall back into place as he settled himself over her, coating her cream over her nipple. He then licked it off and drew her taut nub into his mouth, suckling the sensitive tissue. He didn't let up until her hands slid through his hair and her leg had come off the cushion to wrap around his waist.

"I need more, Derek," Tessa murmured, arching into him as he slowly reached down and finally removed her pink thong. He continued to press his lips against her skin, leaving a trail of kisses in his wake. He once again wrapped his fingers around her ankle and lifted her leg until she kept it resting on top of the cushion. He pushed her other leg so that her foot rested on the floor. This gave him unrestricted access to her core, which was bare of any hair. Her large, swollen clit was easily visible between her glistening labia. "Yes."

Tessa had reached over the end of the couch, clutching the armrest as he settled in and spread her folds with his fingers. She cried out once more when he drew his tongue over her clit, licking away her cream. She tasted just as sweet as the sugar she'd put into her tea. He continued to circle the engorged tissue, every now and then suckling and nibbling until she was writhing underneath him. He nowhere near had his fill of her.

The evening had just begun.

"I'm not going to stop until you come ever so sweetly for me, Tessa," Derek said, sliding his middle finger into her pussy. The warmth of her sheath welcomed him, wrapping tight around his digit. He curled his knuckle so that he was stroking her sweet spot, before using his thumb to rub her clit as he lifted his head to watch her response. "I want my name to be the one that falls off your lips when you do."

CHAPTER EIGHT

TESSA WAS FLOATING on cloud nine, and the only thing she could hear was the sound of her own erratic heartbeat. Her body had come alive under Derek's touch in a way that she'd never experienced before. Derek had found that mythical sweet spot that she'd searched for herself over the years, and he'd found it with one stroke of his finger. Only he didn't stop, continuing to stroke that blissful area until her body no longer understood where she was or how she'd gotten there.

This must be what she'd always heard was possible and had begun to doubt truly existed. No man had ever made love to her so completely or for such a long period of time.

Nothing had ever felt so good, so exhilarating, and so damned sensual that Tessa was afraid she'd literally explode if she couldn't have it again. Every nerve in her body had been awakened and there was nothing she could do but await the outcome of his continued petting.

And then Derek pressed his thumb harder against her clit until lights exploded behind her eyelids, and the sound of her own blood rushed through her eardrums as if a dam had let loose.

Tessa soared, and she wasn't so sure she ever wanted to land.

By the time she could draw air, relax her muscles, and focus her sight, Derek was lying beside her. He gently pulled her into his arms, even shifting their bodies so that she was on top of him. The couch didn't provide them too much room, but they made do. She closed her eyes and savored the security his embrace provided. *This* was something she never could have hoped for in her wildest dreams.

Nothing existed outside the two of them.

"It's a good thing I have off for three days," Tessa murmured, stroking her fingers over his bicep. She'd noticed right away that Derek had a tattoo on his right arm of a beautiful angel with the most stunning wings. The artist hadn't known it then, but he'd captured what Tessa had just experienced...and her wings were still spread to accept the freedom his lovemaking offered. She turned her head and rested her chin on the back of her hand, meeting his dark gaze that somehow made her even warmer. "It's going to take that long to recover."

Derek's rich laugh coated her nerves like molasses, and she suddenly realized one night wasn't enough. He was here for another week. A week of this would surely kill her dead. That should be more than enough time to work him out of her system through immersion therapy.

"We're going to need to take this in the bedroom if you plan on formally consummating this encounter," Tessa said softly, running her thumb over his bottom lip. Who would have thought a man of his virility could have such soft lips? There had been no doubt he knew how to use them, along with his very talented tongue, but she hadn't expected to soar so high. "I have—"

"Is this what you're talking about?" Derek asked, holding up a foiled wrapper with a half-grin. Maybe it was a good thing he had the angel tattooed on his arm. She offset his devilish intentions, but sometimes it was a good thing to be prepared. "I have us covered for the first round."

First round? His declaration shot another streak of arousal through her inner sexual goddess, and she leisurely took the condom out of his hand. They wouldn't be needing it quite yet. She had other ideas on her mind now that she could form coherent thoughts once more.

"We could still make our way into the bedroom though," Derek suggested, his fingers tangling in her hair as she started to slowly make her way down the length of his body. His chest was a solid mass of muscles that led down into abs that could very well be made of titanium. She doubted he would find that amusing, but it was the truth. She trailed her fingers over his warm skin, following behind with her lips and tongue. He tasted and smelled all male, with a hint of that outdoor fragrance she'd come to love. "Or not. Here's good, too."

Tessa set the foiled package on the back of the couch for easy access, leaning up so that she could unfasten his belt. She took her time tugging the leather through the metal fastener, enjoying the view. If the bulge in his pants was any indication, he was very well endowed and more than ready for what she had in mind.

Derek apparently wasn't as patient as he pretended to be, for he leaned up and captured her lips while taking over the removal of the rest of his clothes. She'd had to move to the inside of the couch so that he could finish, but she was right where she wanted to be by the time he'd concluded stripping off his clothing.

"You've certainly grown up, Derek Spencer." Tessa traced the outline of his cock, admiring his length and girth. She'd already lowered herself to her knees onto the floor between his legs, tracing her fingers up and down his thighs. His entire body was in perfect physical condition, and he could have easily made the cover of a fitness magazine. "I like this version of you."

She closed her lips around the tip of his cock, gliding her tongue downward on the underside. It was amazing. He actually tasted like the wild outdoors, too. She couldn't get enough of him. She took him to the back of her throat, not surprised when his fingers became tangled in her hair. He'd want some aspect of control. The prickly sensation on her scalp only further added to her already heightened awareness.

"We should—" Derek's words were cut off by a guttural groan. Tessa had taken her right hand and palmed his sac, giving him a gentle massage as she continued to take him in and out of her mouth. She'd gotten into a rhythm and was pleased to know that she could affect him in such a manner. She used her left hand to wrap her finger and thumb around the base of his shaft as she concentrated on suckling the tip of his cock. It was then that he suddenly took away her advantage. "Come here."

Tessa wasn't sure if he'd learned those moves in the Marines, but she was no longer on the floor. In fact, Derek had somehow managed to shift them so that she was unexpectedly lying on the couch like she'd been before. Only this time, he had donned a condom and was lifting her right knee to give him better leverage. The tip of his cock was suddenly resting at her entrance.

"Impatient much?" Tessa tsked with a half-knowing smile. She didn't mind at all. Her body craved him. She needed more of him and was beginning to question whether a week would be enough therapy to quell her desire. That thought was pushed aside as he ever so slowly pressed his cock past her entrance. "Derek, take me."

"And miss my chance of relishing this exquisite moment?" Derek leaned down and pressed his warm lips to her neck, somehow enveloping her entire body in the same temperature. How was that even possible? He'd started a fire, and she didn't know if it was even extinguishable. "Not a chance."

Inch by delicious inch, Derek slowly guided his cock inside of her. He filled her in a way she never thought possible. He didn't stop until they were truly connected...one. They were one. She suddenly lost her ability to speak.

Her moist sheath stretched around him, accepting his width and length equally. She'd parted her lips to release a small gasp of wonder, but he captured a kiss instead. He'd taken her right hand, lacing their fingers together as he ever so gradually withdrew his shaft until only his tip remained. He then thrust back inside of her, causing her pussy to grasp his cock in anticipation of another stroke.

Derek dipped his head, capturing her left nipple in his mouth. The innumerable impressions upon her body was just too many to absorb. Tessa's mind started to drift away from her body in that enraptured manner he seemed to elicit with just the stroke of his tongue. It was the tiny nip that had her arching her back, wanting more...needing more.

"Faster," Tessa whispered urgently, gripping his

fingers tighter as she brought her right knee up farther alongside his waist. "Harder."

Derek used his knee as leverage, increasing the pace of his thrusts. Her clit was now throbbing in time with her heartbeat, bursting with minuscule explosions every time his pelvis rocked forward. She didn't know how much more pleasure she could take without—

"Oh!" Tessa suddenly found herself on top of Derek. He'd positioned them so that he was sitting on the couch, her knees on either side of him. Never once did they lose their connection, and now his cock was pressed even deeper up inside of her. She had to be one stroke away from an explosive release, but his hands were wrapped around her waist. He was holding her still as he tried to even out his breathing. She could swear his dick was throbbing in time with his heartbeat, the pulse beating against her sheath. "I-I need to come."

"And you will. Many times," Derek whispered, keeping one hand on her waist while sliding the other up so that he was holding the back of her neck. Their foreheads rested against each other, but her body couldn't be that still. She started to move her hips, grinding against him and savoring the minor sparks of arousal, knowing there was a massive explosion to come. "I want you to crave it more than you need to breathe, sweetheart."

Derek's declaration, coupled by the fact that he finally released his hold on her waist, was enough to engulf her body in flames. No man had ever spoken words that could literally replace his touch. She suddenly couldn't draw enough air, but it didn't matter. Her body needed that elusive release she craved.

Tessa rose herself up on her knees, sinking back down with a force that took her by surprise. Her knees trembled as glimmers of that indescribable orgasm began to accumulate in her core. He must have known, for he pressed his thumb against her clit and began to firmly stimulate the engorged tissue until all thought fled from her mind in a rush. The nodule of nerves instantly caught fire and engulfed her entire body.

"That's right, Tessa," Derek whispered against her ear as her pussy contracted around his cock like a vise. "Come for me."

Nothing was putting out the raging flames consuming her. Tessa continued to utilize every bit of strength she had left, slamming his cock into her over and over. He didn't try to tame her in the least, allowing her to dig her fingernails into his shoulders as she took her pleasure. It was hearing her name fall from his lips that fueled the intensity, capturing both of them in the uninhabited blaze. She gathered her remaining breath to scream his name.

CHAPTER NINE

D EREK STOOD IN the doorway wearing only his formal black pants, holding a wooden tray that contained a plate with two pieces of French toast covered in syrup with powdered sugar sprinkled over them. Next to the white porcelain dish were two cups of coffee and a small bowl of fresh, homemade fruit salad he'd cut up from Tessa's selection in the kitchen. He leaned against the doorframe as he took another moment to come to terms with what happened last night, willing the tension to leave his body.

He'd been honest with Tessa from the very start. She understood that he had to go back to his unit in Afghanistan, leaving him only one more week at home. He'd accepted the limits he could provide to any woman a long time ago. This time was no different...only harder.

Why, then, was he still here?

Tessa's bedroom held the faintest scent of her perfume, but it was enough to beckon him to enter. Derek couldn't resist the welcoming fragrance. He pushed off the doorframe with his shoulder and stepped over the threshold. He fought the impression that he'd actually crossed into something more than a mere room. It was her lair.

Tessa was still in the position he'd left her in—lying facedown in the middle of the bed covered in rumpled sheets while her long black halo fanned out over her pillow. Her hand was tucked underneath her cheek as the sunshine kissed her bare shoulder. She was sleeping peacefully, and he'd contemplated leaving her a note upon awakening, going so far as to thank her for last night and promising to keep in touch before walking out her front door. The thing of it was…he couldn't bring himself to do that. He found that he could barely leave her bed to make them both some breakfast.

He'd gone and fucked himself and his heart over by allowing himself to be with his childhood's unattainable beauty. She was his personal version of a unicorn.

Derek couldn't prevent himself from reaching out, tenderly moving a flyaway strand so that it blended with the others. Maybe it was time to make some concessions, without altering too much of the original agreed upon provisions. He didn't question why his chest tightened at the fluttering of her long lashes. Searching for an answer he didn't want would get him nowhere.

"Good morning," Derek murmured, waiting for her blue eyes to focus on him. Her instant, warm smile thawed his soul. She rested the back of her hand over one eye, peering up at him in drowsiness and curiosity. "I have your coffee."

"That deserves a kiss." Tessa's tone was slightly hoarse, still filled with sleepiness. That didn't stop her from rolling onto her back and then scooting up against the pillows, tucking the sheet under her arms. Was that for warmth in the air-conditioned morning chill, or was that for modesty's sake? Her blue eyes brightened upon seeing the contents of the tray. "Oh, my! French toast and fruit, too? Those might deserve more than a single kiss."

Derek gently set the tray over her lap, making himself comfortable by resting his elbow on the mattress, effectively trapping her legs underneath his arm. She didn't seem to mind his gaze as she reached for her coffee and brought it to her lips. Her lashes drifted closed as she savored the ideal java he'd sweetened with sugar and masked the bite with cream. Her expression of satisfaction reminded him of how she looked when she'd taken him in her mouth last night…

He cleared his throat, reminding himself that they needed sustenance before any further physical activities could commence. And there could be quite a few of those, considering how many condoms remained in the box they'd torn open during the night. Derek used the fork to break apart a corner of one of the pieces of French toast before lifting the delicious morsel to her mouth. It was easy for him to distinguish that her lips were still quite swollen from their pleasurable endeavors.

"Hmmm." Tessa slowly chewed her food before swallowing, as if she were contemplating something. He finally dragged his gaze away from her rosy lips, only then noticing she was studying him. She asked her question before he could divert her attention. "What made you stay?"

Derek did admire her ability to cut to the chase. He sunk the prongs of the fork into a cut piece of strawberry before taking a bite of the sweet, red fruit he'd sprinkled with sugar and tossed with the juices of the other fruits. It gave him time to ponder the same inquiry he'd asked of himself upon awakening. He still didn't have an answer, so he had no choice but to go with the truth.

"I don't really know." Derek carefully set the fork down on the plate, making sure the silverware didn't dip into the syrup. He then reached for his cup of coffee before settling back into his previous position to drink his morning joe. "Do you want me to leave?"

His question had obviously surprised her. She took another sip of her coffee, giving herself time to think of a proper response. It appeared that last night had thrown them both into the deep end. There was a simple solution though, because the end result wouldn't change.

"I don't leave town until next Sunday," Derek quietly reminded her, studying her expression for any sign that she wouldn't be interested in the time he had left. "I'd like to continue to spend time with you while I'm in town."

"I'd like that very much," Tessa replied softly, setting down her coffee mug in exchange for the fork. She cut a small piece of French toast with one of the four spines and then smeared it in the excess syrup. She used the edge of the plate to catch the lone drip of the sweet molasses and then slowly lifted it to his mouth. He took the offered bite, though his appetite wasn't for the food on the plate. "Your parents will be—"

"I've already called my parents. Dad is doing fine, and the day is already lined up with endless visitors," Derek divulged, unable to wait any longer to appease his craving for what only she could give him. He removed the tray, along with its contents, placing it on top of her dresser. He'd removed his pants before his knee ever made contact with the bed. Her light laugh enveloped him as he pulled her underneath him, and she eagerly wrapped her arms around his neck to accept his kiss. "I told them I was going to be spending the day with you, getting caught up on old times."

"Then what are we waiting for?" Tessa whispered, drawing him down until their lips met. The sweetness of the syrup was easily discernable and somewhat addictive. "There are many things we should be catching up on, Derek Spencer."

"I couldn't agree more, sweetheart."

TESSA WASN'T READY for the day to end, but Derek had promised his parents he'd be home for dinner. She had turned down his invitation to join them. It was a very sweet offer; however, she didn't want to overstep her bounds when they both knew this…whatever this was…would end next weekend. That was okay though, because she was very, very satisfied right at this moment.

"Tomorrow?" Derek inquired, his lips still pressed against hers. He deepened their kiss though, so she didn't answer for some time. He finally pulled away before brushing his thumb over her sensitive lips. He hadn't shaved since yesterday morning, and a light five o'clock shadow had developed. She liked it. A lot. "How about breakfast before taking a drive out to old man Ackerman's farm? We can ride the trails on horseback and maybe even enjoy a picnic."

"I'd love that more than you could imagine," Tessa murmured, raising up on her tiptoes for one more kiss. Why couldn't she get enough of him? "Drive safe out there."

Derek stepped down before turning back around, a concerned expression crossing his handsome features in place of the satisfaction that had been there earlier. Reality was now returning, and she wasn't ready for it.

"Lock the door behind me," Derek directed in a rather abrupt tone, resting his palm above the doorbell as he continued to give her instructions. He was worried about her, but the day had gone by without incident. Granted, they'd spent most of their time in bed. Nonetheless, nothing had happened. "Should you feel unsafe for any reason, Tessa, you call me without hesitation."

"I will," Tessa promised, resting her shoulder against the doorjamb as she wrapped her arms around herself. She'd honestly forgotten everything that had occurred, even last night's restroom episode. She certainly didn't want to ruin the time they'd spent together last night or today. "Don't worry. You know, it could have just been a prank gone horribly wrong."

Derek looked like he was going to argue, but instead he stepped forward and kissed her one more time. She readily accepted and then couldn't help but gaze after him as he strolled away with his tuxedo jacket slung over one shoulder. She smiled when he turned and continued walking backward with a cocked brow.

"I didn't hear that deadbolt turning," Derek called out, coming to a stop and sliding his free hand into his pocket. He pulled out the key to his rental car and swung it around his finger while waiting patiently. He really wasn't going to leave until she was safely locked inside her house. It warmed her to know that he cared, and she pressed her fingertips to her lips, blowing him a kiss. "Good girl."

Wow. Those two words had Tessa very close to calling Derek back into her house, but she closed the door before she made a fool of herself. She twisted the deadbolt into place and then turned around so that her back rested against the hard wood. So, this was what happiness felt like…but only for a week.

One week. That was length of time agreed upon, and she wouldn't be the one to ask for more. She could accept that. She pushed off the door with a smile.

Tessa dug her phone out of her purse before she made her way into the kitchen. She was starving and had decided she would have the leftover lasagna she'd made two days ago. She quickly swiped the display on her phone, calling up Kate's number and initiating the call.

Straight to voicemail. Damn it. Tessa took off the saran wrap before shoving the cold plate into the microwave. She then concealed it with a plastic cover so that the sauce wouldn't splash all over the inside. One minute and fifty seconds on the timer gave her time to try and call Rae. Her voicemail picked up.

Where was everyone?

Tessa slid her phone onto the granite countertop as she retrieved a fork from the silverware drawer. She needed to talk with someone, but then again, maybe this was fate's way of telling her that she shouldn't share too many details of what had occurred. Maybe Derek wouldn't want her telling everyone they were going to be briefly involved for his short period of leave at home.

Tessa's thoughts drifted over the last twenty-four hours, recalling every caress, kiss, and orgasm that had taken place. Her body still tingled and it amazed her that it still hadn't been enough. They'd spent time telling each other about their lives in more detail than just the cursory impersonal facts, delving deeper and really getting to know each other. How could someone she'd known most of her life suddenly become someone she didn't want to live without?

Ding. Ding.

Tessa was startled when the microwave wasn't the device chiming, but her phone. She automatically reached for it, only to stop short. What if it was the same person who had called her on Thursday? What if they were aware she was home all alone? She was hesitant about looking at the display, but she couldn't help herself. Maybe it was Derek.

It was then that her heart fluttered upon seeing his name, the text immediately initiating a smile. Damn, but she had it bad. She needed to restrain herself and face reality, but she could do that tomorrow. Right now, she apparently had plans for later this evening, and she couldn't be happier that she had this weekend off.

Change of plans. I'll be back at twenty-three hundred hours with a bottle of wine. Have the wineglasses ready...and yourself well-rested.

CHAPTER TEN

THREE MORE DAYS. Tessa tried not to focus on that number as she made her way across the parking garage to where her car was parked. Her twelve-hour shift had gone over by about two hours, and she was practically dragging her feet. Sleep wasn't on her agenda, though. Derek was already at her house, most likely sleeping in her bed. She planned on waking him up with a little more than just a kiss.

Tessa wanted to take advantage of every piece of sand left in the hourglass. She never would have thought that her life would have changed so drastically over the last five days. There hadn't been a moment of her spare time that she hadn't spent with Derek, and she didn't regret a single second...not one. He made her laugh at the most foolish things, he warmed her heart with just a smile, and a simple touch from him lit her soul on fire. She was a completely different person, and he'd opened her eyes to what she'd been missing.

Screech!

Tessa's steps faltered at the high-pitched squeal. The

keys in her hand jangled as she quickly palmed them in response. A slice of anger shot through her as piercing fear consumed her body. She hadn't once thought of Bennett or the events that had happened prior to the reunion, because everything had gone quiet. She'd rationalized that the string of events hadn't been related at all, just as Derek had done the same after days had gone by without incident.

She now forced herself to even out her breathing as she took in her surroundings, trying to explain away a noise that could have come from anything or anyone in a hurry. No one was around at four o'clock in the morning. Even the security guard was most likely in his booth near the exit. No other sound was heard, and she forced herself to pick up her pace, quickly making her way to the left of the garage where her vehicle was parked in the far row.

It wasn't surprising that Tessa would be taken off guard at a noise that advertised someone else's presence. She'd lowered her defenses. She'd spent almost every non-working hour with Derek, who would then in turn spend his time with his family while she was on duty at the hospital. Her schedule had worked out for the both of them, but had it been a detriment to her welfare?

Tessa finally reached her car, immediately pressing the appropriate button on her key fob. The blaring click of the opening locks ricocheted off the other vehicles and around the open space. It was still a somewhat comforting sound. It meant security.

Unfortunately, she wasn't going to be able to close herself inside her car. She wasn't going to be able to lock the doors so no one could get inside. She had been so busy looking over her shoulder that she'd been too preoccupied to see what was directly in front of her.

Blood.

Blood was dripping down the side windows of her car, but the red, sticky substance wasn't what scared Tessa most. It was the one word message left behind that somehow spoke volumes and let her know that she hadn't been wrong in assuming she was in trouble. She *was* in danger. And apparently, it was only a matter of time before this person took these somewhat innocent pranks to an entirely different level.

Soon.

DEREK SLAMMED HIS car door, frantically searching for the one woman who had literally almost caused his heart to fail. His mother almost had someone else to cry over in a hospital bed. He'd never experienced such panic as when his cell phone rang, answering only to hear Tessa's terrified voice coming over the line trying to tell him something about blood, her car, and the fact that someone wanted to kill her.

"Tessa!"

Derek had spotted two uniformed police officers and the security guard. He jogged up the small incline, finally catching sight of Tessa's blue scrubs she'd left for work in yesterday afternoon. Her pale features and the manner in which she was holding herself caused his chest to tighten in a torrent of emotion, but foremost was relief that she was physically unharmed. He didn't have to make his way through the three men blocking his way, for she had immediately ran forward into his open arms.

"I wasn't imagining it, Derek," Tessa whispered in a somewhat stilted tone. She was thrown off balance, but it wouldn't be long before she developed that fighting spirit he'd seen the night of the reunion. "Someone is after me."

The driver's side window confirmed Tessa's declaration. *Soon.* What the hell did that mean? The blood had somewhat dried, if it even was blood. It could very well have been paint, but it was in that moment that he'd caught the slightest scent of copper in the air. Damned if it wasn't blood.

"What do you have?" Derek asked Officer Gusten, who was now facing them with his square features practically set in stone. It was easy to make out his nametag. The other policeman had turned away and was talking into the mic attached to the shoulder of his uniform. Derek held Tessa close as he continued to ask his questions. This had to be resolved before he went back to Afghanistan. "Have you checked the video surveillance?"

"We have," Gusten confirmed, unclicking his pen so that he could slide it back into the pocket of his uniform. "The incident occurred around ten o'clock last night, right at shift change of the guards. Unfortunately, the perpetrator was dressed in all black and had one of those ski masks covering his or her entire face."

"His or her? The camera couldn't even make out a shape?" Derek shot a quick glance over at the security guard, who didn't appear in the least fazed by the fact that this misconduct had happened at the beginning of his watch. "You can't tell by the size of the body?"

"The security feed is recorded in black and white, making it hard to decipher the figure of the assailant, especially considering the manner in which the camera was angled." Officer Gusten tapped the small notepad he held in his hand against his other palm as he addressed Tessa. "Ma'am, I'm aware of the other circumstances you reported over the last month. You mentioned previously you thought Bennett Harris might have something to do with them. Is that still your understanding? We'll speak with Mr. Harris to confirm his whereabouts last night, but is there anyone else you think could have done this?"

Tessa shook her head, her fingers pressed against her pallid lips. It was all she could do to keep it together, and

Derek could sympathize. She'd dealt with this harassment basically on her own for over two weeks, only to have everything stop when they started spending time together. She wouldn't have expected what had transpired tonight, so she was entitled to be a bit shaken.

"Someone had access to a lot of blood, which would indicate it's most likely someone from inside this hospital. Could we see the video footage?" Derek inquired, wondering if there was something about the aggressor that Tessa could identify, maybe something in their mannerisms. She was familiar with a good portion of the residents in Catfish Creek. Chances were good, especially considering what had taken place at their high school reunion, both of them knew the identity of her pursuer—someone from their graduating class who worked at the hospital. But why? What could his or her motive be in tormenting Tessa? "There might be something in his or her bearing Tessa recognizes."

The security guard looked over at Officer Gusten for approval, who was already nodding his head in confirmation. Derek wanted a moment alone with Tessa before they followed behind, so he let them know they would follow along shortly. He then drew Tessa back into his arms, savoring the fact that she hadn't been hurt and making a silent promise to see to it that it stayed that way.

"I've got you, sweetheart," Derek murmured softly

against her temple. "We'll figure this out quick."

"Will we?" Tessa asked harshly, resting her forehead against his chest. He rubbed her back as she wrapped her arms around his waist, going over their options. "This person keeps getting closer and closer to me, but I have no idea who they are or what they want."

She had a point. What did her pursuer want? There had been juvenile incidents with vague threats that amounted to nothing. He and Tessa were missing something vital that could no doubt unravel the reason she was being targeted.

"Let's go look at the video footage," Derek insisted as he wrapped an arm around her shoulder, guiding her to where the two officers and security guard were waiting for them. "We'll then sit down and go over every single detail of what's happened, mapping it out the way we would process raw intel on an insurgent or terrorist. The answer is right in front of us, Tessa. We just have to look for it."

CHAPTER ELEVEN

D EREK WAITED UNTIL thirteen hundred before ascending the stairs to Tessa's bedroom. He'd held her until she'd finally fallen asleep, which she'd fought against with every fiber of her being. Fortunately, exhaustion had taken over, and her body had eventually succumbed to slumber. He would check on her before going back to the list he'd been cross-referencing—their graduating class versus the hospital staff.

It hadn't been easy to find the employee directory. He ended up calling in a favor from another Marine who had gone through advanced training at Dam Neck, Virginia. In his capacity as an 0291 Intelligence Chief, he had access to virtually every business server inside the United States without leaving a trace of his passing. The relationship between most businesses and the military had started decades before with ARPAet—the infancy of the Internet. Hospitals, along with other businesses, had been eager to have their information computerized and networked in a secure manner.

Access was key, and Derek had people in position to

look at virtually every digitized word on every server in the country. The information they needed wasn't technically classified, but it was proprietary to the hospital and protected by access.

Once his friend had a copy of the directory, Derek simply copied the file across and emailed it to his own Gmail account. Now came the hard work of deciphering what information might benefit them.

Derek quietly made his way into Tessa's bedroom by silently pushing open the cracked door. She was in the exact same position he'd left her at zero seven hundred. Her brow was still creased in worry, though she had a flush to her cheeks that signified her color was finally returning. He resisted the urge to reach out to her, not wanting to wake her. She'd already informed her supervisor that she wouldn't be on shift this afternoon, so there was no reason for Tessa not to catch up on her sleep. He turned to head back downstairs when her fingers wrapped around his wrist.

"Have you heard anything?" Tessa inquired softly, her blue eyes searching his for any sign of information. He had nothing to give her and regrettably shook his head in response. "Do they know where the blood came from?"

"No, but that much blood didn't come from a simple cut. The police are checking access logs and video surveillance for the blood bank and morgue." Derek laced his fingers with hers. He would have sat on the edge of the bed, but she scooted over and drew him down until he was lying next to her. "Sweetheart, why don't you try to get some more sleep? I'm going over a list of hospital employees against those from our graduating class. It shouldn't take too long to compile a list of people for the police to question."

Tessa had lifted his arm so that she could lie against his chest, wrapping her arm around his waist. She snuggled against him, her body warm from being cocooned in the sheets. Derek understood about needing a timeout every now and then, and this moment was hers for the taking. He held her close, offering her comfort and security.

What would happen come Sunday when his flight departed for the first leg of his flight back to the UAE for briefing and then into country?

It wasn't something Derek could look forward to, knowing her life was in danger. The police would have to figure out who was responsible and succeed on their own in putting the culprit away for a very long time.

"Make love to me," Tessa whispered, sliding her hand up the front of his shirt until her soft fingertips met his neck. He closed his eyes and prayed for strength, not wanting to take advantage of her while she was in this state. "Please."

"You had a really bad scare today, Tessa," Derek

consoled, pressing his hand tenderly against hers. He leaned up on his elbow, causing her to roll on her back and look up at him with those blue eyes full of earnest. She was going to be the death of him. "Let's try to figure out who—"

"Whoever he is, he's proven that he's not going away," Tessa said with a bite of anger. She apparently didn't want to talk about what had taken place this morning, for she leaned into him so quickly he had no choice but to use her momentum for both their sakes. Her hair fell around the two of them, isolating them from the afternoon sunshine coming in through the blinds. "I need you inside of me, Derek. Please don't make me beg."

He didn't hesitate. How could he? He rolled her back so that he had room to undress, which also gave her access to the nightstand. She had ripped the foil and had the condom ready before he even got his pants off his legs. Her sweet voice professing her need made him hard as a rock, but he wasn't the type to fuck without properly working both of them up to the point where nothing would satisfy them except each other. She had other plans and it was all he could do to remain leveraged above her while she rolled on the latex.

"What you do to me…"

Derek didn't even bother finishing that sentence. Tessa had already wrapped her long legs around him, ready and waiting for him to take her. He thrust forward and stopped, needing a moment to adjust to the overwhelming pleasure. Damn, but she took his breath away.

"Don't stop, Derek," Tessa murmured in his ear before she nipped at his lobe. She had no idea what she was asking. He could literally lose himself in her, and it was all he could do to hang on to some semblance of sanity. "Fuck me hard like you want me."

Whether it was the plea that fell from her lips or the fact that she'd sunk her fingernails into his back, he didn't know. But he gave her what she wanted.

Derek pulled back and lunged forward hard enough that the bedframe slammed against the wall. There would be one hell of an indention in the drywall, because he didn't stop. Her warm sheath was wet with her cream, and his cock couldn't have fit better if they'd been made for one another. He drove into her over and over, hearing his name fall from her lips before her pussy contracted around his shaft.

He wasn't even close to being done. He used his knees as leverage as he continued to thrust inside of her, leaning down to take her nipple in between his lips. She arched her back to make it easier, exposing her neck in the process. He eventually bit her shoulder lightly after he'd had his fill, once again feeling her legs tighten around his waist indicating she was starting to come.

Tessa's reaction reminded him of when he'd bring her to pleasure with his mouth, and she couldn't help but close her thighs around him until she could relax her muscles. It was an endearing trait and one that was specific enough to her. Just thinking about her uninhabited reaction to his touch had him driving his cock into her and holding still, finally savoring his explosive release.

"What you do to me…" Derek trailed off, repeating what he'd said before. It was the truth. He gradually pulled out of her, disregarding her attempt at keeping him on top of her. His weight would eventually become too much. "Come here."

Tessa didn't argue, but instead went willingly into his arms. She nestled against him and no more than five minutes passed before he sensed her muscles relaxing. Eventually, her breathing evened out, and she fell into a deep sleep. This time, it wasn't so restless.

Derek stared at the ceiling in futility. All his carefully laid out plans had vanished like a puff of smoke. He'd warned himself early on that this brief relationship had to come to an end before his emergency leave ended. It had to. Only he couldn't bring himself to disengage in a manner that would be in both their best interests. The truth of the matter was that he didn't want to end things here.

There was still so much more between them to be

explored. Tessa had come to mean so much to him in such a short amount of time. But how could they sustain any semblance of what they'd managed to create this past week? He accepted the blame, and he would have to deal with the consequences come Sunday. The military didn't give a pass just because he'd let his guard down and fallen for a woman who lived thousands of miles away from where he would be stationed.

Derek held her for close to twenty minutes before he reluctantly untangled himself from her arms, tucking her in nice and tight so she didn't lose that secure feeling. He quickly snatched his clothes up off the floor and then cleaned himself up in the bathroom. He checked on her one more time before forcing himself to return downstairs to finish going over the list of names he'd been given.

It was time to end this reign of terror that had descended upon Tessa. He didn't have a choice but to be on that flight out to New Bern and then a short drive down to MCAS Cherry Point, where he would catch a resupply transport out to Dubai, but he did have the ability to put this scumbag out of business and make sure he was apprehended and put behind bars.

"YOUR HUSBAND IS just fine, Mrs. Spencer," Tessa reassured Helen, covering the older woman's hand.

Derek's mother had called them at nine o'clock this evening to say that she was taking his father to the emergency room. It had turned out to be nothing more than gas pains from the amount of greens she'd introduced into Ben's diet, but it had been a scare nonetheless. "They're getting his release papers ready now."

"Oh, please call me Helen," she murmured, leaning into Tessa. "I can't thank you enough for how kind you've been this evening."

Tessa gave the older woman a hug while looking over to where Derek was standing next to his father's stationary gurney. It was as if he'd known her eyes were on him, for he immediately glanced up and met her gaze. His expression was unreadable. Was he regretting bringing her with him to the hospital? He'd mentioned that it wasn't safe to leave her at home, but that wasn't the reason she wanted to be here. She just hadn't had the courage to tell him that little tidbit.

"I heard that multiple victims were brought in from a car accident, so it could be a while before those release papers are signed. Why don't I go and get us some tea? I happen to know a nurse's lounge who has the best Earl Grey Tea this side of Abilene." Tessa loved the soothing drink herself and always made sure she had some on hand during her shift on the cardiac floor. "Do you take cream?"

"Oh, that sounds lovely," Helen exclaimed, patting Tessa's hand in appreciation. Derek's mother seemed more stressed by tonight's events than she had upon her husband's surgery. That was to be expected, especially considering she'd had time to think about what her life would be like without Ben. They'd been married over thirty years. Losing that type of love was unthinkable. "Thank you, Tessa."

She quietly slipped out of the room, leaving her purse behind. There was no need for it where she was going—her home away from home. She spent more hours here at the hospital than she did at home, and she figured it would become even more so given the fact that Derek would be leaving soon.

All of a sudden, it was as if Tessa couldn't get enough oxygen. She stopped in the long hallway and leaned against the wall to catch her breath. Derek was leaving, and she most likely wouldn't see him again for a very long time, if ever. He was going back into combat. The physical ache was unexpected, and she was glad she hadn't been in the room when it hit.

Derek had been nothing if not honest about where he stood in regards to what he'd wanted out of this week, and she more than agreed to his terms. It had been what she'd wanted as well. Now? He'd come to mean more to her than any casual fling.

The sound of the elevator chiming grabbed her attention, forcing her to finally move from where she'd been frozen. She pressed a hand against her chest, hoping it would ease the tightness that had coiled inside of her. Numerous ways of how Sunday could go flashed in her mind, each one with the same ending.

She would be left alone.

Tessa forced her legs to move and carry her forward until she eventually stood in front of the elevator doors. She pressed the button that would take her up to the cardiac wing, grateful she had some time to herself. She had no choice but to accept the fact that Derek was heading back to his deployment overseas, and it was up to her to ensure that their friendship stayed intact. She wouldn't cry, she wouldn't break down, and she certainly wouldn't ask for more than Derek could give her. She would somehow find the courage to say goodbye.

CHAPTER TWELVE

"**M**OM, DID TESSA say she was going to the restroom?" Derek asked, walking around his father's bed to the set of chairs that were positioned up against the wall. Spending hours in the emergency room hadn't been the way he'd planned to pass this evening, but he wouldn't be anywhere else. His parents had needed him, and he was just grateful that he was still here to be a support system for his mother. He hadn't thought twice about bringing Tessa, but that didn't mean he wasn't worried about being in a building that most likely held the person responsible for her troubles. "I told her she shouldn't go far, especially considering the police haven't been able to close her case."

"Tessa went to get me a cup of tea," Helen said, her sparkling brown eyes telling him that she had something more she wanted to say. She stood and placed her hands on his arms, just like she used to do when he was little and she wanted his attention. "Derek, she is just lovely. I knew the moment I set the two of you up to attend the reunion that there would be a connection. She is—"

"Mom, don't do this right now," Derek cautioned, shaking his head upon hearing his mother's advice. "It isn't the time."

"And when will that time ever come?" Helen asked, sharing a look with Ben, who was listening intently to what his wife had to say. He didn't appear so inclined to disagree with her either, leaving Derek in somewhat of a difficult place. "Will it be next year when you finally decide to come home? Or will you reenlist with the Marines for another four or five years? Honey, we are so proud that you've served your country, but you aren't in a field that would afford you a life outside of your profession. You're always on deployment, your focus is always on your current mission and your fellow Marines, and your life is always in harm's way. When do you make time for yourself?"

Derek ran a hand through his hair in frustration, taking a step back from his mother. He needed the space. What he didn't need was his mother telling himself something he didn't already know. He had many choices ahead of him. Yes, some of those even needing to be addressed before he flew out on Sunday, but not right this minute.

"Tessa shouldn't be going anywhere in this hospital alone, not even to go get tea," Derek said, sidestepping his mother's lecture. The only thing that mattered right now was keeping Tessa within his line of sight. He hadn't been able to make one connection between the high school graduates of 2007 who had been at the reunion and the list of hospital employees. That didn't mean there weren't a lot of staff who had been graduates of Catfish Creek High School. There were, and quite a few at that. It didn't change the fact that none of them would have been invited to the masquerade ball unless he or she were invited by a classmate who graduated with them, and that alone opened up a whole spectrum of possibilities. "You stay here with Dad. I'll be back in a moment."

Derek opened the heavy door, immediately noting that Tessa wasn't in the hallway. He gritted his teeth together in frustration, knowing full well she wasn't safe in these corridors. Someone had made it his or her mission to threaten Tessa to the point of police involvement. The initial ante had already been raised, so what made her think she was safe wandering around inside of this building?

She would have used the elevator versus the stairs considering the cardiac unit was on the tenth floor. It was the only place that he knew of where she would go to get tea, unless she went to the cafeteria. She'd mentioned numerous times that she kept a stash of Earl Grey Tea in the nurse's lounge, so Derek gambled and headed toward the elevator banks. Maybe he could catch her before she ran into any trouble.

Unfortunately, Tessa was nowhere to be found. Derek jabbed the button with the arrow pointing upward a little harder than necessary, but he didn't like that time was running out and there was nothing he could do to slow it down.

Derek also didn't like the fact that his father had spent the evening in the emergency room. That frantic phone call from his mother hadn't been expected, and all his thoughts had centered on the possibility that this could be the end of a life...one who wasn't done living. It was like whiplash to see his father clutching his chest in pain, only to be laughing at something the nurses said an hour later. All that told Derek was that life was fleeting. Luck could change on a dime, so maybe it was time for him to cash in his chips with the Corps.

The elevator doors swooshed open, though Derek had to wait to enter as a family of four exited. It didn't take long to reach the tenth floor, though he wasn't quite certain of the location of the nurse's lounge.

"Excuse me," Derek said, interrupting two nurses who were on duty. He recognized the older woman from his father's time here, though she'd never been assigned to Ben's room. The other nurse must be the one who was filling in for Tessa this evening. "Have you seen Tessa? She's getting tea for my mother."

"No," Margaret said, shaking her head after confirming with the other nurse that she hadn't seen Tessa either. "I haven't seen her since last night."

"She must have gone to the cafeteria then," Derek mused, nodding his head in appreciation. "If you do happen to see her, would you please send her down to the emergency room? My father's about to be released, and we're going to be heading out soon."

"Of course," Margaret replied with a smile, though it faded slightly when she rested her hand on the tall counter in concern. "How is she after last night? We couldn't believe what had happened, especially after her being so excited to be formally offered the position."

"I'm sorry?" Derek must have missed something. Tessa hadn't said anything about being offered a position, though he was aware that Margaret was talking about the nursing director position. Tessa had mentioned the opportunity a few times, but she hadn't known when a decision was going to be made. Of course, last night's events had taken the spotlight off such a remarkable announcement. "Are you saying Tessa was awarded the position?"

"Yes, she was told at the beginning of her shift yesterday." Margaret turned to another nurse who had called out to her. It appeared her small break was over and that Derek would have to get more information from Tessa about such a momentous career incentive. "It's a shame we were all too busy yesterday to celebrate. I'll have to get the girls together for a small celebration at

The Grange."

"I'm sure Tessa would love that," Derek replied, already turning on his boot to head back to the elevator bank. He called back over his shoulder, "Thanks, Margaret."

It took at least another five minutes before Derek had entered the cafeteria. That was more than enough time for Tessa to have gotten a tea for his mother and returned to the emergency department. Sure enough, she was nowhere in sight. He would have called his mother before coming this far, but she was one of those people who followed the rules. He'd literally seen her take her cell phone and shut it down so that she couldn't receive any calls…just as the sign had instructed.

"Hey," Derek greeted upon entering his father's room. His dad was already dressed and sitting sideways on the bed with a somewhat tired smile in place. Helen was standing next to him, reading the very fine print of his release papers. Unfortunately, Tessa wasn't in attendance. "Did Tessa not come back? She wasn't up on the cardiac floor, and I just came from the cafeteria."

Helen and Ben exchanged worried glances, both of them shaking their heads in response.

"No, son," Ben replied with concern, automatically reaching for his wallet that had been set on the rolling tray. Helen didn't object in the least, quickly folding the papers she'd been given and shoving them inside her purse. "Could you have missed her? Are you sure she wasn't up in the nurse's lounge?"

No, he wasn't sure, because he'd taken Margaret's word for it that Tessa hadn't been by the nurse's station. Damn it. Derek turned back to the door, pulling on the handle and waiting for his mother and father to join him before giving them specific instructions.

"Would you please go back to the cafeteria? Ask any personnel you run into if they've seen Tessa." Derek joined them out in the hall, all three of them heading in the same direction. "I'll go back upstairs. Mom, turn your phone back on in case I need to reach you. Call me with updates, and I'll do the same."

Derek veered off once more at the elevator bank, slamming the button so that it lit up. He'd known the second Tessa had left his father's room that something wasn't right. He should have immediately called out to her, but he'd thought her intention was to use the restroom across the hall.

"Come on, come on," Derek muttered, watching the lighted display above the doors in earnest. Had Tessa's stalker finally made his move? Was she in danger, or was he making something out of nothing? Maybe she was simply making his mother a cup of tea. The knot in his stomach told him otherwise, and his instincts had never steered him wrong. The doors finally drifted open and he found himself once again ascending in his search for Tessa. "I'm coming, sweetheart. Just hold on."

CHAPTER THIRTEEN

TESSA STARED IN horror at the syringe that could very well end her life. She struggled to swallow against the fear that had constricted her throat, but what choice did she have but to try to talk sense into the woman who had made her life a living hell for the past three weeks.

"Jackie, why are—"

"Don't," Jackie practically screamed, holding the syringe like one would a knife before swinging it upward, only to stab someone with all her might. God only knew what type of drug was contained inside the long plastic barrel, but Tessa was one hundred percent sure she didn't want to find out. "Don't pretend that you're all innocent. You knew I needed that position, and yet you accepted it anyway. I warned you over and over to just leave, but you couldn't take a hint."

This was not the same Jackie Bauer who Tessa had grown up with. Granted, she'd graduated a year after Tessa, but they'd both been cheerleaders. They'd both attended the same events, the same parties, and basically had hung out with the same crowd without ever actually becoming close friends. That was kind of hard to do back then, especially after Tessa had left to attend nursing school. The woman standing before her was not the Jackie she'd grown up with. This woman was a psychotic version of the girl she'd known.

"Jackie, there were quite a few of us who were up for that position," Tessa said, trying her best to use reason. She had her hands up in mock surrender, but it didn't seem to make a difference. Jackie all but had her cornered in the nurse's lounge, which had little traffic this time of night. "I-I didn't know you wanted it that bad, s-so why don't we go and speak to Lydia? She's the one who—"

"All you had to do was move to Florida like your parents wanted you to do." Jackie seemed to be talking to herself more than she was to Tessa. "It was a good offer. You could have been next to your parents. I would have become Nursing Director here. The other nurses are mediocre at best. And then Derek showed up, causing you to think you could have something here. I heard the two of you talking at the reunion. I heard him say he was thinking of coming back and that's when I realized I would have to do something more to change your mind. I should have just killed you in that damned restroom."

"Look, we can go and—"

"*We* aren't going to do anything," Jackie cut in on

Tessa's plea. "I tried to take care of this weeks ago. You know, you're really fucking stupid for someone supposedly so smart. I mean, you were offered a job in Florida where your parents live, and one who anyone in their right mind would have accepted. Why is it that people like you get everything you want, and I end up with nothing?"

"People like me?" Tessa asked, trying her best to stall Jackie from doing something she would regret. Harassment was one thing. Murder? "Jackie, we practically grew up together. You don't want to do this. The authorities will look at everyone and know that you—"

"The authorities won't even connect me to your sudden heart attack. I'm just a distraught coworker," Jackie wailed, indicating how she would come across to the police. Her despondent features changed in the blink of an eye to one of rage. "I did everything in my power to make sure you left Catfish Creek, but you were just too dense to see what was right in front of you the whole time. The best thing I can do is end this right here and now."

Jackie gestured toward the door with the syringe— the one Tessa couldn't stop staring at in shock—and explained how she thought she could get away with murder. The terrifying thing of it was…she could.

"It's so sad the way Tessa died." Jackie's head was tilted, and she was speaking in a voice that mimicked what would be said after the other nurses found her body. It amazed Tessa that this woman was able to bring tears to her eyes within seconds. She was truly psychopathic. "She was so young to go into cardiac arrest. She—"

"That's right," Tessa confirmed, having no choice but to push Jackie's buttons. What other alternative was there at this point? "I'm in perfect health, so you know the authorities will conduct an autopsy. A healthy woman just doesn't drop dead like that, Jackie. Think this through."

"Oh, I've thought this through." Jackie sidestepped the small kitchen table to block off Tessa's attempt at reaching the door. She brought herself up short. "It's my turn to have everything, Tessa."

This couldn't be happening. Tessa had done everything she could to keep Jackie talking so that someone—anyone—would come through that door. Margaret was on shift, and she was always sneaking her way into the lounge for more coffee. There were numerous other employees who used the lounge as well, but no one had even attempted to come into the room. This was *her* floor. She should have been safe here. She'd left Derek downstairs, thinking she would only be away from him for five or ten minutes. Jackie was trying to make it last forever.

Tessa could sense that her attempt to stall Jackie had

slowly dwindled down to this precise second. It was odd. She would have thought she'd be a quivering mess, but her fight or flight instinct had kicked in...and she wanted to fight. She had too much live for and hadn't realized how much of a coward she'd been until this very moment.

Tessa was going to fight.

Jackie lunged forward, but Tessa had already anticipated her movement. Adrenaline coursed through her body, and she instinctively kept the table between them as she lunged for a knife someone had washed in the sink. The blade was pointing toward her. She had no choice but to grab it and keep moving, but there was no way in hell Jackie was going to allow her near the only exit.

Tessa succeeded in quickly shifting her weight and bending her ankles, barely managing to miss Jackie's downward swing with the syringe. She didn't stop her forward momentum either. She persistently kept advancing, leaving no choice but for Tessa to shove the chairs in her wake. She kept stumbling backward while trying her best to keep the table between them.

"Jackie, stop!" Tessa cried out, hoping like hell someone heard her through these thick walls. "Someone! Help!"

Tessa was finally able to get a proper grip on the knife, and she held it out in front of her, swiping sideways when the syringe in Jackie's hand came a little too close. The woman's anguished cries echoed around the room, but it was Derek's voice that penetrated the pulsing whoosh that had taken up residence in Tessa's eardrums. He was too late, and it was more than apparent that Jackie had locked the door. She'd been sane enough to think this through, but she hadn't counted on certain unexpected variables.

Tessa had taken the evening off, and she'd spent it with Derek and his parents. It had been a fluke that she'd ended up in the lounge at the same time Jackie had, unknowingly walking into a trap. They'd both made mistakes, but it was Jackie who would end up paying.

Jackie's face contorted with rage as she stopped in her tracks to stare at the door. It was clear she was going through her options. There were none.

"It's over, Jackie," Tessa said, unable to hide the tremor of fear in her tone. She raised her injured hand, not realizing the extent of the damage done by grabbing the knife by the blade from the sink until now. Oddly enough, it didn't hurt. All she was aware of was the relief washing over her at the knowledge that this hell she'd been going through the past few weeks was finally coming to an end. "Look at me. No one is going to believe there wasn't a struggle of some sort."

"Then I have nothing to lose."

Tessa wasn't sure what she'd expected. Maybe she

thought Jackie would concede and put down the syringe, facing whatever charges the police filed against her. Or maybe that she would collapse to the floor in tears, asking for forgiveness. This entire confrontation had been surreal, but it was nothing compared to what happened next.

It was if she was having an out-of-body experience. The strangled, anguish cry that came out of Jackie's mouth was something Tessa would never forget. She did the only thing she could at the forward attack and turned her body while holding up the knife in an attempt to defend herself. The blade sunk deep into tissue in a manner she hadn't experienced since her days in nursing school when she'd worked on a cadaver. Both of them abruptly froze upon the end result.

The gurgling Jackie emitted from her throat turned Tessa's stomach. She glanced down to find the blade of the knife inserted deep below Jackie's sternum, the woman's hands resting over Tessa's. Where was the syringe? Where was it?

Tessa stepped back in panic, but it was as if her body finally registered all the stings and aches that had accrued over the past twenty minutes. The palm of her hand throbbed where the cut was still bleeding and her shoulder stung as if she'd gone a round or two with a bumble bee. She glanced down through the tears to see the syringe sticking out of her shoulder.

"No. No." Tessa tried to see if the contents of the barrel had been injected, but she had to blink several times to clear her vision. "No."

DEREK COULD BARELY hear Tessa's plea through the heavy door, but he believed beyond a shadow of a doubt that her life was in danger. Someone on the inside had thrown the deadlock, and chances were it wasn't by her own hand.

"Margaret!" Derek yelled the woman's name, the only one coming to mind that would have access to this room. "Margaret! Where the fuck are you?"

Derek started going room to room, not caring that he was barging in on someone's privacy. Tessa needed him. He had to reach her as soon as possible.

"Margaret!"

"What's wrong?" Margaret said in somewhat anger that Derek would be causing such a disturbance on her floor. She had appeared from down the hall, a frown marring her tired features. "Why are you yell—"

"Tessa's locked in the nurse's lounge. I need the key."

"What do you mean she's—"

"Margaret, I don't have any time to waste," Derek barked out, reaching for the keys that were attached to her wrist on one of those elastic spiral bracelets. "Call security. Go! Right now!"

Derek didn't waste any time and ran back down the corridor, taking a shortcut through the deserted nurse's station. He tried three keys before locating the right one, flipping the deadbolt to gain access to the room. He shoved the door with his shoulder and took in every detail of the bloody scene before him without stopping.

Jackie was on her knees, holding a hand to her bleeding stomach. Tessa was three feet away with a bloody hand hovering over some type of syringe that was sticking out of her shoulder. Chairs were overturned, the table had been shifted toward the counter, and blood was smeared over the floor in numerous areas.

Jackie Bauer. Jackie had been the person responsible for the constant harassment, but what would have driven her toward attempted murder?

"Tessa," Derek called out to her softly, not sure why she hadn't pulled the needle out of her arm. He reached for her, but she jerked away in panic. "Tessa, look at me. What was in the—"

"I-I can't see, Derek." Tessa had looked up at him with tears in her eyes, her lashes beating furiously to erase the moisture away. "Is there anything inside the barrel? Is the syringe full or did she…"

"It's full," Derek reassured her, but he afraid to touch her or the syringe. Honestly, he was terrorized for the second time in a short time span that he could lose someone he loved. And he did. He loved Tessa with a passion, regardless that they'd only gotten reacquainted seven days ago. It was hard to control his heart rate or his thoughts as he tried to figure out what his first move should be. "It's full. Can you take it out? What's in it? Do you need me to get Margaret or—"

Tessa jerked the syringe out her skin and through the fabric of her shirt, keeping the barrel tight inside the palm of her hand. Derek's chest tightened at what could have happened had that red liquid entered her body. Her blue eyes were crystal clear and now filled with contempt as she held up the needle in accusation. She tried to take a step forward, but he stopped her. He didn't want her anywhere near Jackie Bauer.

"You were willing to kill me for a fucking job?" Tessa barely got the words out in such a harsh whisper filled with a variety of emotion that the rough undertone hurt his ears. He reached for her, not allowing her to pull away. He tucked her in close and held her, both of them looking on as Margaret knelt before Jackie to see how badly she was injured. "What kind of monster are you?"

Jackie was now sobbing uncontrollably and staring at her hands the entire time Margaret tried to get her to lie back. Security guards rushed through the door, one of them having been at the crime scene last night. He had already whipped out his cell phone, no doubt calling the police.

They would want the evidence contained, so Derek

motioned that they would need some type of cap and bag to secure the syringe. The security guard was still speaking into his phone while searching the drawers for something that would work.

It was over. It was finally over, and Tessa was safe. She'd come out on top, and her life was no longer in danger.

"It's over, Tessa." Derek held her against him until she finally accepted his declaration. A sob caught in her throat, and she wrapped her arms around his neck. "You're okay. You're safe."

"I want you to come back to Catfish Creek." Tessa pulled back far enough so that she could look up at him, her sincerity and hope shining through. Something shifted inside of him and a warm peace settled over his heart. "I want you to finish your contract and then come home. Come home to me, Derek."

EPILOGUE

TESSA TIREDLY LIFTED the strap of her purse to settle on her shoulder as she glanced up at the illuminated numbers counting down each floor. On one hand, filling in for one of her nurses had been a change of pace. It had been exhilarating to go back to her roots. On the other hand, the demanding hours had made her appreciate her position as Nursing Director all the more. She would be glad when her unit was back to full staff.

She tilted her head back against the elevator wall, closing her eyes in exhaustion. All she wanted to do was go home, crawl into bed, and sleep until tomorrow morning. She'd just worked her fourth twelve-hour shift in a row with the intention of having four days off because...

Derek was finally coming home.

She'd dreamed of him every night.

She'd imagined him holding her, touching her, and loving her.

And now?

He was coming home to her.

They had spoken nearly every day since he'd left to go back to Afghanistan, either by phone or over FaceTime. She would gently trace his features on the computer monitor with her fingertips, memorizing each and every line so she wouldn't be lonely when she closed her eyes. He'd somehow become her everything.

There had been very few days where Derek hadn't called her. Those had been the worst days of Tessa's life, terrifying and graphic images of what could have happened playing over and over in her mind. On rare occasions, the military had programmed communications blackouts on their end. It always coincided with the Marines taking casualties in country. It never failed to cause a fear stronger than the day she'd almost died at the hands of Jackie. It was in those times she realized just how much he'd come to mean to her. She would gladly give her life to guarantee his.

Tessa peered through the lashes of one eye to see how many more floors she needed to descend to reach the lobby of the hospital. Two more. She exhaled in sleepiness and pressed her cool hands to her face, needing to stay awake long enough to drive home. She was to pick Derek up at the airport in less than seven hours, roughly giving her six hours of sleep. That was more than enough knowing that tomorrow night she would be sleeping in his arms.

The ding of the elevator indicated she'd finally

reached the main floor, where all she had to do was walk around the corner to enter the parking garage. She gave herself a pep talk about putting one foot in front of the other, reminding herself that she would soon hear Derek's voice telling her that he was about to board his plane in Virginia to come home. He'd been back in the States at Quantico, processing out of the Marine Corps for the past two weeks. She'd waited an entire year for this homecoming. She could wait seven more hours.

The doors swooshed open.

Tessa thought for just a second that she'd fallen asleep. The scene before her was something that could only be conjured up by a dream. She blinked again, but nothing changed.

Derek was no more than eight feet from the elevator bank, kneeling on one knee with a small box in his hand. Her mind was still not accepting the mind-blowing view, so she let her eyes drift behind him to find that both her parents and Derek's were holding up a very large white sign with the words *Marry Me* written in big, black letters.

Why were her parents here? For that matter, why were his?

It was after midnight.

No one should be here.

Derek shouldn't be here. He was supposed to be driving to the airport.

The doors ever so slowly closed, erasing the view that had her literally speechless.

"Shit," Tessa muttered, rushing forward and dropping her purse in the process. She didn't care. She pressed the button that would reopen the doors over and over and over, willing for the elevator to open. "Shit, shit, shit. Open, damn it!"

And just like that, Tessa was rewarded once more with a view that she would forever commit to memory. More people had gathered around, but it was only Derek who remained clear in her now blurry vision. She furiously blinked the tears away. She didn't want to miss a single second of the next few minutes.

The doors once again tried to drift shut, but Tessa stepped forward to stop it from happening again. She wasn't sure how she succeeded, considering her knees were trembling. She somehow had closed the distance and was now looking down at the one man who was her everything.

"Tessa Marie Daniels, I have thought of nothing else but this moment for the past three hundred and sixty-five days," Derek said softly, his words for her ears only. "I have no intention of leaving your bed once I'm lying beside you this evening, and if my mother taught me anything, it was to be an honorable man."

"Then we shouldn't disappoint her," Tessa laughed lightly through the tears that had gathered in her eyes.

She'd thought of their future often—a short engagement, a very long marriage, two spoiled children, and maybe one or two more furbabies. She had already adopted a six-year-old mutt who she loved with all her heart, and Milo would enjoy having more company, either in the form of four legs or two. As for her? She'd waited a long time for this moment. "Our parents already know I love you, Derek Spencer. My answer is yes. Yes, yes, yes."

Derek quickly stood with that charming smile of his and gathered her in his arms, tilting her over his arm and capturing her lips for a kiss to celebrate her answer. He'd already known that she would say yes, yet he'd gone to all this effort to include both his and her parents. Why? Because he loved her, just as she did him.

Their parents, plus the hospital staff who couldn't pass up such a romantic scene, gathered around. There was applause, whistles, and congratulations being thrown about, but she only cared about one thing…

He had finally come home to her.

~ THE END ~

A Bad Boy Homecoming

Thank you so much for reading **Honor**! Derek and Tessa's story is about that one crush in high school that was just out of reach...and about returning home after being gone for so long. A lot can change, but then some things will always remain the same. Each book within the Bad Boy Homecoming series is written as a standalone, though there are beloved character crossovers that I think you will enjoy revisiting as you read through the series. If you enjoyed the book, we'd love if you could please leave a review to show us how much! Reviews help authors every day, and we truly appreciate it.

Thank you for joining us in this Bad Boy Homecoming reunion, and we hope you'll not only find a romance you love, but a few authors as well.

Happy Reading!

The Books of Bad Boy Homecoming:
Dropout by Carrie Ann Ryan
Trouble by Avery Flynn
Prom Queen by Katee Robert
Honor by Kennedy Layne
Rock Star by Stacey Kennedy

About the Author

First and foremost, I love life. I love that I'm a wife, mother, daughter, sister… and a writer.

I am one of the lucky women in this world who gets to do what makes them happy. As long as I have a cup of coffee (maybe two or three) and my laptop, the stories evolve themselves and I try to do them justice. I draw my inspiration from a retired Marine Master Sergeant that swept me off of my feet and has drawn me into a world that fulfills all of my deepest and darkest desires. Erotic romance, military men, intrigue, with a little bit of kinky chili pepper (his recipe), fill my head and there is nothing more satisfying than making the hero and heroine fulfill their destinies.

Thank you for having joined me on their journeys…

Email: kennedylayneauthor@gmail.com

Facebook: facebook.com/kennedy.layne.94

Twitter: twitter.com/KennedyL_Author

Website: www.kennedylayne.com

Newsletter:
www.kennedylayne.com/newsletter.html

Books by Kennedy Layne

Surviving Ashes Series
Essential Beginnings (Surviving Ashes, Book One)
Hidden Ashes (Surviving Ashes, Book Two)
Buried Flames (Surviving Ashes, Book Three)
Endless Flames (Surviving Ashes, Book Four)
Rising Flames (Surviving Ashes, Book Five)

CSA Case Files Series
Captured Innocence (CSA Case Files 1)
Sinful Resurrection (CSA Case Files 2)
Renewed Faith (CSA Case Files 3)
Campaign of Desire (CSA Case Files 4)
Internal Temptation (CSA Case Files 5)
Radiant Surrender (CSA Case Files 6)
Redeem My Heart (CSA Case Files 7)

Red Starr Series
Starr's Awakening & Hearths of Fire (Red Starr, Book One)
Targets Entangled (Red Starr, Book Two)
Igniting Passion (Red Starr, Book Three)
Untold Devotion (Red Starr, Book Four)
Fulfilling Promises (Red Starr, Book Five)
Fated Identity (Red Starr, Book Six)
Red's Salvation (Red Starr, Book Seven)

The Safeguard Series
Brutal Obsession (The Safeguard Series, Book One)
Faithful Addiction (The Safeguard Series, Book Two)
Distant Illusions (The Safeguard Series, Book Three)

Are you ready for more of the Bad Boy Homecoming series? Check out the next romance in our sexy reunion standalone series:

ROCK STAR
by Stacey Kennedy

This book contains an excerpt from the forthcoming book Rock Star by Stacey Kennedy. This excerpt has been set for this edition only and may not reflect the final content of the forthcoming edition.

CHAPTER ONE

T RAVIS WALKER MADE women's panties disappear.
     On most nights, anyway.

Tonight, sitting on a wooden stool set upon the stage at Catfish Creek high school's conference center, only one woman was on his mind. His fingers strummed over the strings of the guitar, mouth rested near the microphone, and after he sang the final two lines of the chorus—*I wanna kiss you under the moonlight. And love you 'til the sun comes up*—the applause from the crowd reopened his eyes.

Sparkling string lights and masquerade masks hung from the ceiling above him, reminding him that he wasn't surrounded by thousands of his typical screaming and wild fans. In his Texas hometown, he stared out at teachers, old friends, and classmates, all dressed in formal wear and masquerade masks.

From his seat in the spotlight, he recalled playing for smaller crowds on this very stage back in high school. Those had been some of the happiest days of his life. Now, fresh off his last world tour, he realized he loved that scene, too. The energy of a smaller crowd, who knew him personally, and a larger crowd, who thought they were in love with him, was so different he couldn't compare the two, but admittedly, he missed the intimacy that came from a smaller venue.

Done with his song, and with the crowd quieting, he slid the guitar strap over his head and handed the instrument back to a member of the band that'd been hired to play at Catfish Creek high school's ten-year reunion. He jumped off the stage and sighed in relief, finding that all the cell phones pointed in his direction were now put away, and the flashing lights were gone.

That's when he set his focus on what mattered to-night: finding *her*. Rae Evans—the muse behind his song, *Moonlight*.

He scanned the crowd overtop the decorated tables with their gold chairs, but the beauty had escaped him somehow. He recognized Annie Flowers, the librarian, who gave him a little wave, and Christopher Christian-son, the principal, who was grabbing a drink from the bar. Travis could have sworn he spotted Rae entering the masquerade ball when he'd begun his song. Desperation now clawed at his chest.

Determined to find her, he moved farther into the crowd, just as his cell phone vibrated in his pocket. Knowing exactly who it'd be, and that he couldn't ignore the call, he reached for his cell phone and then frowned at the text from his manager, Scott Price.

Nice job. The video is already up on YouTube. Fans are loving it. The mask was a nice touch. Don't miss your flight in the AM.

Travis shifted the black mask around his eyes, and the muscles along his shoulders tightened with the reminder of the weight they carried; of the need for him to always be on point, and the fact that nothing, not even his high school reunion, was sacred anymore.

Life had changed dramatically since the last time Travis had stepped foot into the community center. But he didn't want to think about the shit weighing on him, so he fired off a response—*I'll be on it*—then tucked his cell phone back into his pocket.

He had tonight, and he wouldn't waste it.

In the eyes of his manager, Travis had come to the reunion to put on a show and to look *real* to his fans. But Travis hadn't come for the publicity; he came for one very good reason: to find his anchor—the woman who stopped his world from spinning wildly out of control.

Again, he searched the crowd, ignoring the way some men glowered at him, and some women batted their lashes. *Rae.* That's whom he'd come here to see tonight. Only her.

The band behind him started playing another ballad,

and that's when he found her, staring right at him from across the room. She wore a sleek, black, strapless gown with matching long, black gloves.

His muscles surged with adrenaline, and he went to move toward her when a hard voice came from behind him.

"Karly wants you to play another song."

Travis slowly glanced over his shoulder to find the biggest asshole in Catfish Creek high school history. Jason was once a buddy Travis had hung out with. Rae, Travis's high school sweetheart, was best friends with Kate, and Kate had loved—and later married—the dipshit behind him.

Times had changed.

Travis didn't owe Jason anything now, and he certainly didn't owe the reunion's event planner, Karly, shit. "You can tell Karly that I told her I'd play one song, and that's exactly what I did. Bother me again, and we'll have a problem."

Jason didn't make a move or say a word in rebuttable. Once a coward, always a coward.

Pulled by the energy only Rae conjured, Travis stretched out his fingers, shedding his frustrations as he moved with purpose through the crowd. Her pretty, hazel eyes surrounded by dark makeup followed his every move, and she yanked him forward with a simple look.

He'd seen her every so often on the Internet, when

the Catfish Creek newspaper featured her for her charity work, and also on the website for the vet clinic she owned. She'd always been a pretty girl, but she'd grown into a blindingly beautiful and stunning woman. Her gown fit her like a glove. A gold-speckled mask somehow made the creaminess of her skin appear richer. She wore her shoulder-length, brown hair in big waves framing her round face.

She didn't look so fresh-faced and innocent. Tonight, she looked sexy as hell, and Travis's cock swelled eagerly at her beauty.

When he reached her, the air felt charged between them. "Rae," he said.

Her eyes warmed. Dark red, painted lips curved. "Travis."

Christ, he remembered how those lips tasted. How *she* tasted—every goddamn inch of her.

Beneath her mask, those pretty eyes now turned a little suspicious. "I wasn't expecting to see you here tonight."

"Well, to answer you, I need to tell you a story." He offered his hand. "How about we dance, and I'll share it."

For a second, he thought she might refuse him. She simply stared at his hand. The tightening in his chest eased when her eyes met his again and she slowly slid her palm into his. He closed his fingers around hers and sensed her soften, making him smile. He vividly remembered the way she used to melt so easily for him.

Reliving that infectious energy she carried, he led her into the middle of the dance floor, then he spun her around and pulled her into him, nice and close, sliding his hand across her lower back.

She laughed softly, eyes twinkling behind her mask. "You've still got the moves, I see."

Her honest smile warmed the cold parts of his soul. "My moves will never fail me." He grinned.

The band played the perfect song. Something straight off the 2006 *Top 100* charts. A little sexy and slow, keeping her hips swaying perfectly with his, he did nothing to shield his erection. But one look into her eyes told him that was all right. With her breasts pressed against his chest, her cheeks a little pink now, he noticed the heat in the depths of her gaze. He'd recognize it anywhere. That heat felt like it belonged to him—always had, always would.

"How long are you staying in town?" she asked, in an obvious attempt to divert their attention away from his cock.

"Just tonight." He stroked his thumb over the back of her hand. "I fly out bright and early in the morning."

"Only tonight?" She shot him a questioning glance. "You came all the way here from New York just for the reunion?"

"You seem surprised."

She shrugged, seemingly unaffected when another couple bumped into her, her interest obviously centered on him. "Seems like a long way to come for only a few hours."

A very good point, indeed. "Well, you see, that brings us to my story." He sent her out, twirling her around before bringing her in close again and returning the smile she gave him. "But I think we need to go back even further for you to truly understand."

"Go on," she said, watching him closely.

He paused, collecting his thoughts, then he began. "You'll never hear me complain about my life. I have far more than I probably deserve."

"That's a good thing," she said firmly, even if a playful grin teased her lips. "You have a pretty amazing life, and you'd better not complain to me about all the amazing trips you get to take around the world, or you might lose a tooth."

He chuckled but leaned in, calling her out. "And how do you know so much about my life? Reading up on me?"

"A little," she admitted.

That's what he liked most about Rae. She was honest, through and through. The fact that she followed his life could bite him in the ass later, but at this point, there was no going back, so he pushed conversation along. "So, then you know that I have a very good life. I travel. I stay in fancy hotels. I eat at amazing restaurants. I never have to lift a finger. I have everything that anyone should want."

Her eyes searched his. Then, "But it's not the life you want?"

Of course, she caught on. He didn't expect otherwise. "It's not that I don't want the life I live," he explained gently. "It's that something is missing. Something very important."

"Which is?"

"You."

She began nibbling her lip like she used to do in high school when she became confused. "Me?"

"Yes, you." He slid his hand along her spine, pulling her in closer, leaving no room between them. "I can have anything I want, Rae. There is nothing that's not available to me. But what I had with you...I haven't had that since."

Her eyes softened, and her voice grew quiet. "That's really kinda sad, Travis."

"It is what it is." He shrugged, not wanting to get stuck on the things he couldn't change. That wasn't why he came to the reunion. "My manager told me that I'd been invited to the reunion and saw it as a business opportunity. But I saw it as a personal one."

The song shifted to something faster, and the crowd

began to fill the dance floor, bumping into his back. He refused to let her go, holding her tightly against him. "Do you want to know the real reason I came to the reunion tonight?"

"Yes," she said, a little breathlessly.

"I came to relive the past, Rae." He released her hand, wrapping his other arm around her and bringing his mouth close to hers. "That's the only reason I'm here. We have this night. That's it." He was encouraged by her shiver. One that spoke of her willingness to give him all that he wanted and more.

Hot and hard, he dropped his head into her neck, inhaled the subtle hints of her flowery perfume, and said into her ear, "We have a chance that many people don't get. Do you remember how good we were together? How intense things were between us? Have you had that since?"

"No," she rasped.

"It's tempting, no? To go back and feel what we felt before?" He dragged his nose across her neck in the way he knew she liked, feeling her quiver under his hands. "That's why I'm here, Rae. I want to remember what we gave up." He brushed his lips across her neck, and a soft moan escaped her mouth, as he murmured, "I want one more taste of you."

She gasped and stepped back, blinking rapidly. "I...I need to get some air." Then those pretty pink cheeks and wide, excited eyes were gone, her dress trailing behind her as she ran for the door.

Travis shoved his hands into the pockets of his suit and grinned. He didn't mind hunting her, it sweetened his reward.

Distant Illusions
(The Safeguard Series, Book Three)

Follow along as USA Today Bestselling Author Kennedy Layne takes you down a suspenseful path where a ruthless killer is always one step ahead…

Brody Novak has been given his first assignment for Safeguard Security & Investigations, and it has nothing to do with his lead role as a communications specialist. With the rest of the team occupied on a hunt for a serial killer, he's the only one left behind to handle what everyone thought to be an open and shut case. He should have known it wouldn't be that easy.

Remy Kinkaid has faithfully made a phone call once a month for the last four years to ensure the killer who murdered her sister remained behind bars. Every time she's been given the same answer—except today.

Brody and Remy must work together to hunt down a murderer, despite their growing attraction. It isn't safe to give in to their desires, when the killer is always one step ahead of them. It's only when he stumbles that Remy is finally given the opportunity to face her past in order to have a future.

www.ingramcontent.com/pod-product-compliance
Lightning Source LLC
Chambersburg PA
CBHW061240170626
46809CB00007B/2753